Spring 2024

Publisher: Sinister Wisdom, Inc.

Editor & Publisher: Julie R. Enszer

Guest Editor: Alison Blevins

Graphic Designer: Nieves Guerra

Proofreaders: Mariana Romo-Carmona, Sarah Horner, Margaret Zanmiller

Board of Directors: Roberta Arnold, Cheryl Clarke, Julie R. Enszer, Sara Youngblood Gregory, Yeva Johnson, Briona Jones, Judith Katz, Shromona Mandal, Joan Nestle, Rose Norman, Mecca Jamilah Sullivan and Yasmin Tambiah.

Name of artwork: July 2nd, 2018 | July 6th, 2018
Artist: Juliana Rico
Media: Photographic Composite, Inkjet Print on Metallic Paper
Artist Statement: In California, July tends to be the hottest month of the year. The kind of heat where it can be uncomfortable to exist. This work is part of a photographic series of digital collages entitled *Nothing was Ever the Same.* Every day in the month of July 2018 I attempted to simultaneously work through and escape the concerns that were bubbling up in my life. The issues that were causing me to be overrun with anxiety and depression. The problems that had made it uncomfortable to exist.

These diary entries are unrelated but somehow interconnected to one another. The daily photos often referenced geographical locations, self portraits, and random moments that felt like treasures of the banal. *Nothing was Ever the Same* looks into the subconscious and coping to show that nothing is ever quite as it seems.

Artist Bio: Juliana Rico (she/they) is an award winning, nationally showcased, queer, Latinx, visual artist, educator, consultant, and academic. Her artistic practice utilizes primarily photography and video to investigate intersections of identity including ethnicity, culture, social norms, and the body.

Rico is a passionate advocate for social justice, diversity, equity, and authentic representation in educational and arts & culture spaces. She believes all underrepresented and marginalized groups who have felt unseen no longer have to accept the narrative placed on them; they can write their own.

SINISTER WISDOM, founded 1976
Former editors and publishers:
Harriet Ellenberger (aka Desmoines) and Catherine Nicholson (1976–1981)
Michelle Cliff and Adrienne Rich (1981–1983)
Michaele Uccella (1983–1984)
Melanie Kaye/Kantrowitz (1983–1987)
Elana Dykewomon (1987–1994)
Caryatis Cardea (1991–1994)
Akiba Onada-Sikwoia (1995–1997)
Margo Mercedes Rivera-Weiss (1997–2000)
Fran Day (2004–2010)
Julie R. Enszer & Merry Gangemi (2010–2013)
Julie R. Enszer (2013–)

Subscribe online: www.SinisterWisdom.org
Join *Sinister Wisdom* on Facebook: www.Facebook.com/SinisterWisdom
Follow *Sinister Wisdom* on Instagram: www.Instagram.com/sinister_wisdom
Follow *Sinister Wisdom* on Twitter: www.twitter.com/Sinister_Wisdom
Sinister Wisdom is a US non-profit organization; donations to support the work
and distribution of *Sinister Wisdom* are welcome and appreciated.
Consider including *Sinister Wisdom* in your will.

Sinister Wisdom, 2333 McIntosh Road, Dover, FL 33527-5980 USA

CONTENTS

NEW LESBIAN WRITING

NOTES FOR A MAGAZINE

D o you remember Kris Kovick's collection of comics *What I Love about Lesbian Politics Is Arguing with People I Agree With?* Alyson Books published it in 1991; I read it around the time that it first came out. I was twenty-one. It filled my imagination for the types of conflicts and politics that might enrich my future lesbian life. Elana Dykewomon was the editor of *Sinister Wisdom* then; I never imagined that three decades later, I would be editing *Sinister Wisdom* and encountering lesbian politics and its arguments from Kovick's perspective.

Since our issue about trans people and trans identities in the spring of 2023, I have been thinking about Kovick's light-hearted portrayal of lesbian politics and conflicts. Over the past year, some of the arguments have not felt loving—or like they were with people with whom I agree. Yet through it all, I wanted to maintain my love of lesbians and our politics, and I think I have. What I have also come to appreciate is that what I love even more than lesbians and our politics is the communities of lesbians and queer women that we imagine and create, communities that nurture and sustain us even through the hard stuff.

More than one critic of *Sinister Wisdom* 128: *Trans/Feminisms* has said to me, ominously, *well we will see what the future holds for* Sinister Wisdom. As though chiding me to not be inclusive of trans issues and trans folx and implying that it seems like transpeople have taken over *Sinister Wisdom*. In those moments, I try to smile and think about how much I love and appreciate lesbians, our politics, and our communities.

Sinister Wisdom 132: How Can a Woman Who Is with a Trans Man Call Herself a Lesbian? returns with trans topics, giving voice to lesbians who have trans partners. The issue opens with a stunning essay by Minnie Bruce Pratt from a manuscript titled Marrying Leslie that she was working on at the time of her death.

Minnie Bruce, Allison, and I had talked about her participating in the launch for this issue. Sadly, that is not to be. Yet this issue is another incredible one with contributions from great writers like Kimberly Dark, Mary Vermillion, Suzanne DeWitt Hall, Deanna Armenti, and more. The issue also features a selection of photographs by Jan Phillips and new writing by a range of known and emerging lesbian writers including Alix L. Olson, Jenny Johnson, Liz Ahl, Monica Barron, Janet Mason, Joyce Culver, Nancy Stoller, and more. The issue concludes with remembrances, including a stunning poem by Evelyn C. White.

It is an honor to publish this issue and all the writers in it. While writing this "Notes for a Magazine," I learned that Kris Kovick died in 2001 at the age of fifty from breast cancer. Over twenty years later, her legacy of art and laughter remains.

In sisterhood,

Julie R. Enszer, PhD

Spring 2024

NOTES FOR A SPECIAL ISSUE

Shortly after my diagnosis with MS, my husband began transitioning. We were raising three children together, and our youngest was only a year old. We struggled. But our struggle was mostly with how to navigate my new role as a disabled person. His transition was easy. For me. I wasn't surprised because I knew he was unhappy. I pushed for him to follow this new path. Two years later, I wrote *Cataloguing Pain* (YesYes Books, 2023). The book is a hybrid collection that juxtaposes these two events. For both of us, my illness and his transition are woven together. This weaving is more like tangling at times. Occasionally, we are snarled. I don't know how to understand my body without his body because we've been shattered and remade together over and over. He has been the constant home where my body lands. I can't speak for my husband, but I hope I have been the same for him. For both of us, my identity has been a source of fear. We pass so well has a straight couple. This brings him a sense of peace and me confusion. My lesbian identity has been a major part of my life since coming out at seventeen, so most of my struggle has been with understanding how I continue to fit in our community and how to reconcile identity with perception.

I was thrilled to meet Julie Enszer at the Saints and Sinners Conference in New Orleans in 2022. She had given me, what I consider to be, one of my first "real" publications in 2016, and I've been thankful for that boost ever since. Coincidentally, that poem appears in *Cataloguing Pain.* Kismet. Our brief chat after a panel planted the seeds for this issue. She has been lovely to work with, and I'm so grateful for what she does for our community.

I always research before beginning a project, and then I often seem to set out to write the book that wasn't available for me to read. While it may be true that everything worth saying has already been said, marginalized folks still have a difficult time finding and holding their stories and experiences in their hands. I couldn't find any poetry books about infertile lesbians pregnant through reciprocal IVF when I was writing my first chapbook, *A Season for Speaking*. I was able to access pages of beautiful work by queer disabled folks while writing my most recent books, but the voices of lesbians with trans identifying partners were harder to find. I was honored to help curate some of those voices for *Sinister Wisdom*.

Minnie Bruce Pratt begins the issue. This issue was curated before she died. I will always treasure the gift of spending time with her work and being able to communicate with her about the piece published in this issue. She gave us selections from *Marrying Leslie,* her in-progress sequel to *S/HE*. Pratt's piece must begin the issue because, for many of us, she and Leslie are the beginning. When my husband told me he was transitioning, *Stone Butch Blues* was the first book I suggested he read. The selections in this issue give us a small glimpse into Pratt and Feinberg's relationship. We see the everyday moments, laundry, and conversation. But there is heartbreak, not just for Pratt but for several of the contributors in this issue. Pratt writes, "And I know, yes, I know, reader, that writing this now will never, never bring her back to answer my questions. I know that and yet I keep writing." Tenderness lives in every line.

Mary Vermillion's title "How Can a Woman Who is with a Trans Man Call Herself a Lesbian?" is the quiet question on repeat in my inner monologue and the heart of many conversations between my husband and myself. Vermillion's piece assures me that I'm not alone. And all the voices in the pages of this issue are a chorus of others also grappling with language and labels and identity. I'm not the only person who "hungers for glimpses of women like herself."

Kimberly Dark writes, "I'm old enough that 'femme dyke' means something to me about my own intentionality of gender and sexual orientation." I'm old enough to have proudly worn an

"I like dykes" button every day of college in the late 90s, so I'm comforted that this issue spans generations. Dark and Pratt on the same pages with reuben quigg. This is quigg's first published poem, and he writes, "i've dug my nails hard into living and hung on for dear life."

I'm grateful to all the writers and artists for sharing their work with me. Jessica Dittmore's comics and the collaborative piece by Zoe Cutler and Anne Haddox will surprise and delight. These are pieces I never imagined receiving when we put out the call. Barbara McBane's long form poem is an epic, "a twisting red streak through a white shine." Every piece in this issue has given me comfort and power, shown me strength and humor, and will buoy me through the uncertain currents around all of us.

Allison Blevins
April 2024

SIR AND MA'M

Minnie Bruce Pratt

During our year of getting to know each other for the first time, we have shuttled between our cities, Jersey City and Washington, on the Amtrak train, on the green Peter Pan Trailways buses with names on their brow like "The Lost Boys" and "Tiger Lily."

A Broadway show sings: "Getting to know you, getting to know all about you." But I will never, never know all about Leslie.

I can't even remember now the way things happened that year, exactly when I knew what about us being together, what order we happened in, what I knew before what else I knew.

Naked in bed together, Leslie on her stomach sleeping, my glance traces over and over the luxuriant curve of her long waist rising into her deep full hips. My hands rest on her hardened biceps, her widened muscled shoulders, the inextricable wedding of masculine and feminine.

The complexity of her/hir gender, what she later called "the poetry we each make with what we are given."

When we get off the PATH subway in New York City and walk down the crowded 14th Street working-class block between Sixth and Seventh Avenues, she is *ma'm'ed* by people going into the discount stores at one end of the street and *sir'ed* by people rush-houring out of the 4-5-6 lines at the other end.

When we go out to eat in Adams Morgan in D.C., me facing Leslie, ceiling-high mirror over her head, I watch the flirtatious smiles and nods of the gay male waiter standing behind me as he interprets her gender complications as "gay but passing," as feminine man, a queer in hiding. He silently offers her an amuse-bouche tryst-treat downstairs out back, quick before the main course comes, with me the presumably heterosexual spouse none the wiser.

When we go to the lesbian house party and someone hits the tape deck to start the music, when Leslie takes me in her arms and we slowgrind, butch and femme to Anita, suggestion of female frottage in public, grinding so lightly, pestle and spices, Leslie working so hard, the sweet sweat on her forehead, me trying to find the place, pendulum, where I take my weight back and then give it to her over and over, then I see my lesbian friends shrink back, the distance widens and widens, eventually we are left alone in the room.

People look at us and think they know who Leslie is at a glance. Then they think they know who I am because I am with her.

And they don't they don't they don't know anything at all because every moment we ourselves are making it up, back and forth, back and forth. How do we do this gender fuck sex together, the kiss and the sorrow, the laundry and the travel, up the back staircase of what we've been taught to do.

All the Animals

Sometime in the winter I say, "Let's go to Puerto Rico." Thinking of the little patch of pasture and a visitor's bunkhouse I'd found the year before, from a two-line ad in the hand-typed stapled "Lesbian Connection." Because how do you travel, a woman alone who can't, won't, doesn't want to hang out at the bar late at night in case a man, or in spite of a man. Some dykes in Michigan had been putting out that newsletter for years, from before I was out as a lesbian.

I am thinking of Leslie and me as "lesbians" until I say, "Let's go!" Then Leslie says OK, sounds OK, won't need a passport to go from the U.S., she doesn't have a passport, and her driver's license is iffy, about to expire, and how to get another with the M to match her who people see, so definitely no passport, but the license is good through next year, OK to travel on, but what about them expecting only "women" if it is one of those "women-only" places for lesbians, but if men go there too, then are the bathrooms coded, will she have to take herself out of "woman" to be able to use the bathroom? When it is just her and me being lesbians together?

We don't talk about this all at once, but at some point I write off to the woman who lives there and takes in paying guests at the camp-out pasture and the bunkhouse with the porched kitchen for cooking, and I don't now remember what I said, how did I even explain my question? A very masculine woman"

But the woman writes back and says, no problem, no problem, everyone welcome as they are, and then we are in a bumblebee of a plane propelled from the mainland to Isla de Vieques, La Nena, and then in the rattling straight-shift rental we both know how to drive, bumping uphill over unknown dirt roads in the rapidly-gaining dark, there we are staggering under our borrowed tent we've never set up together, through the unknown weeds and sand out into the pasture with only starlight for our guide, putting our shelter up as if blindfolded, some elaborate survival test that we pass while doubled over laughing, falling into our sleeping bags with our clothes on, then our clothes off, skin to skin, waking up to roosters crowing, heat crowding in on us with the first staring sun. Leslie lying on me, sweating on me, fucking me until I crow with pleasure, and in the middle some huge animal comes snuffling at our edges to see what we are doing. Laughing again.

There is a rain-water, gravity-released cold shower and no gender required anywhere. It's a two-acre paradise, and in the photographs, I have a red hibiscus flower behind my right ear as I smile, and Leslie is smiling on the beach in a bathing t-shirt and shorts, her arms open wide and outstretched to me. We don't go to the luminescent bay at midnight to see the water coruscating with all its tiny beings, but we do go to the west end of the island one midday, and at the edge of the sand there is a tiny pulpo swimming in the rocky shallows, its eight arms busy gathering lunch. So close we could have touched its arms wheeling and whirling.

Then a jeep of men drives up, Leslie hurries me into our rattle-trap and does a three-point getaway in the sand. She is serious about our getting away. They look like GIs off duty looking for something to do, and there we are, available to be done. Who knows who it is they see when they look at us? The island is occupied by the U.S., has been occupied since 1898, and these young white guys are part of an occupying force used to doing whatever they want with whoever is on the island, us or the people who live there or the pulpo in the small, transparent wash of the sea.

Years after us there are waves of demonstrations to fight off the occupation, the pollution the military leaves behind, the leftover bombs. What we see that day when we drive south to have lunch in Esperanza is graffiti on the sea wall: U.S. Out!

On the way back to our refuge, we see another whitewashed cement wall by the road, with all the animals painted, jumping out of a cerulean blue wheel of constellations, a whale, a dolphin, an eagle, a panther and the wild, wild whirling arms of the little pulpo.

When the Rider Comes

Leslie says when she sees me for the first time, I am standing looking down at some political pamphlets. I am reading one of them, "The Roots of Gay and Lesbian Oppression," and she thinks: "There is a woman whose mind rides her body like a rider rides a horse."

When she first comes to visit me, I see her out in my backyard, at the picnic table underneath the apple tree. I walk barefooted over the crispy-dry grass to sit with her, I scoot up beside her, my bare feet on the table. She admires my long legs and I pridefully say yes, strong, strong enough to be good at riding horses, how I loved the power to direct their gait, slant, stop and begin. Then she jokes, "Good at what you do with butches too?" My oblique face, my I-don't-know, my looking away, my not-knowing.

I am waiting for her in a room down a long corridor. I am on the far side of an empty room like every classroom I've ever worked in, sitting in one of those flimsy plastic stackable chairs. I hear the clack-clack of her boots as she walks down the hallway. I am hearing the rider coming.

My destiny, my desire, my fate, my future coming toward me. That which is grander than sexual love, than romantic love.

Here she comes through the door, very serious, toward me down the length of the room, over the worn-down scuffed linoleum. She comes right up next to me and kneels down. We're eye to eye now and she says, matter of fact and questioning: "I think I'm falling in love with you."

And was that before or after she says, "We're acting like we're married. What are we going to do?"

I don't know what I feel. She is so strange and so familiar, a person who seems to be from home, someone who knows me, and someone I've never known before.

Inside me I am hollow. There is nothing made-up in me from my life before that can answer her. There is no love-dazzle, there is no carried-away. It's just me and Leslie, alone in a corridor of events yet to be determined.

I look at her and she looks at me, together in the emptiness, at the beginning of what is not yet.

From Each to Each

To get to know each other, we have to visit, neither of us has much money for the bus or train, but I have more. I am teaching classes by the semester at the university in College Park, while I don't know exactly how Leslie makes enough to pay rent and buy groceries.

She mentions doing data entry sometimes for a medical researcher, and sometimes she has to wear wrist braces because her hands are so sprained. Later, over the years, she mentions different low-wage temp jobs, the ones so low that gender complexity doesn't disqualify her, at least for a while—working in a PVC pipe factory and a book bindery, throwing boxes onto a Borden's assembly line, cleaning out ship cargo holds, washing dishes, serving as an ASL interpreter.

What I know when I visit her in Jersey City, when I stay with her in a little room in the "Summit Soviet," the house on Summit

Avenue that's been handed down as a rental to several generations of comrades, is that I make more money than she does, and more reliably. She has a mattress on the floor, a few clothes, a few books, not enough money and too much oppression to have been able to stay in one apartment for very long, no way to keep much in the way of possessions.

I know what's fair. I have more, she has less, so I say we're going to share our expenses in proportion when we are together, the travel, the food. We should share, from what we each have to what we each need. I have not yet read the Communist Manifesto: "From each according to their ability (to give), to each according to their need."

Sometime toward the beginning she says to me, "I already knew you were not anti-communist. I read what you wrote." That was my outrage at the Greensboro Massacre in 1979, the Klan with cop collusion shooting down union organizers, communists, in broad daylight in North Carolina, six dead and not a single Kluxer convicted. Later I see the graffiti on a highway overpass on the way to Durham: "Be a man, kill a commie." The silent message to me as a white woman: "Don't look. Don't tell."

When I visit in December, she and her roommate Charlie, the doorman, watch grade-C horror movies, the threat-and-alien-invasion black-and-whites of the 50s, the anti-communist cold-war fright of ant armies that horrified me when I watched movies alone in the Ritz Theatre as a girl, the insect hordes that devoured every person in their path until all that's left is the boat floating down river with nothing but shredded clothes and some hanks of hair.

Nothing but wigs! they shout as they watch in the other room, hooting at the scare fiction. In the kitchen I am shredding potatoes to fry up latkes for Hanukkah. When I look in the cabinet for plates, all I find are empty peanut butter jars. There is no food on the shelves, none in the kitchen except what I have bought.

Leslie takes me another night to a communist potluck. Plenty to eat, no one turned away. I meet Rosie, who is like her name in her seventies, a fighter since her teens. I meet Vinnie, another of the oldest comrades, sick, fading, at his last supper and beaming some unspoken approval at Leslie.

Suddenly I am almost back at Wednesday night church suppers at home, without the religion.

The relief that I can be younger, that I don't have to know everything, the brief comfort that I am there with the old folks.

Girl

When we first start living together, I break down late one afternoon because there is no door between the kitchen, where I am doing something, I don't even remember what now, and Leslie's office, where she was talking on the phone.

The line of sight and sound runs all the way through the apartment like railroad tracks. No way to get separate, no way to get quiet. Me sitting on the floor, crying, at the loss of my silence.

Not knowing how to work or live with her so close in.

Then she leaves me. She is traveling in the Midwest, in the South, for what's her job now, being the person who wrote a book.

A wave of sadness, the dry rustling of leaves because of the heat. Grieving. I'm alone in the apartment, in this vast metro-city. I've moved here to be with Leslie and now she's gone. I say to myself that even though I love her and she loves me, I am on my own. I will always be alone, always.

I walk aimlessly back and forth through the apartment. I sit and hem blue twill curtains by hand, sitting on the blue corduroy Goodwill couch I brought from D.C. I see no one I know for the weeks Leslie is gone.

I am frightened by how much I miss her physically, not even so much sexually, but on a deep womb level. Come into me, be in me. I numb myself. When she comes back, she says I look like I've become middle-aged with grief. But I am that age, I am 46 years old.

Then I am the one who has to go away for my job, to be someone who teaches people to write about taboo. The morning

I leave for the airport, Leslie comes downstairs with me and puts me in a cab. I look back, waving until she is out of sight. The driver smiles approval at me, at us: "You'll have to call him, or he will you."

At twenty, I was the girl who wanted both love and respect. Through the twenty-five years since, I've waited for the moment that always comes, when the male husband or the female lover looks at me and their smile slips from tolerant, amused, to contemptuous.

How I tried to smother that younger self so I never saw how people despised me, the girl self.

But Leslie always says to me, "I call you 'Girl!' for an honorific—for being so smart and so brave."

I've always thought of you as yourself, raised a girl, living as a woman, living as a man, living as yourself, true to yourself, my stone butch lesbian trans masculine muscular hilarious funny tender sentimental brilliant revolutionary sexy communist lover.

I loved you because of your gender beauty. The ways you were more than all the pronouns—she, zie, s/he, he, zhe, sie, ze.

I loved the multiplicity, the everything that was Leslie. And never denied the dear secret places that had been hurt and assaulted, never denied anything of who you were.

The Clitoris of Laundry

There are all kinds of moments in learning how to live together. I do the laundry in the basement, one old beat-up slot-machine of a washer, and can't understand why she doesn't take a turn with that.

"Don't think I'm a man because I have fabric dyslexia," she says, and at first it's a joke but then it isn't. And finally it's not exactly a fight but a strain, an exasperation, and she says: "You are talking to me as if you think I don't have a clitoris."

Meaning that I think she is a man, that she is a he who doesn't think laundry is his work. Then she tells me about trying to do laundry for another femme lover, and turning everything pink because she didn't know about reading the labels. She didn't know about reading the labels because her mother didn't teach her, and her mother didn't teach her, because her mother thought something was wrong with her.

That's a whole long other story that I learn over time, about what her mother and her father did to her that meant she left home one way or another very early, and without knowing much about laundry, for instance. There are a lot of other stories that I don't learn at once, that I only learn over time. There are a lot of stories that I never hear, that she never tells me.

Years later, fifteen year later, after she's gotten very sick, and we are stuck in traffic in Jersey City, we were hot and very tired on the way back from walking at the Green Swamp. Wanting to be home and she was impatient with me about something, I can't even remember what now.

A sharpness in her voice, something that hurts my feelings. I tell her I'm suddenly reminded of the man I was married to, my pain at that memory, please don't.

Suddenly the chasm. She is devastated with horror and full of distrust. How could I say that, after all these years?

I kept saying, no, no, not you, my memory, the memory of someone else's anger. She is the one who said to me at the very beginning: "Tell me what makes you feel loved."

Then, twenty-two years after we first met, in the days before she dies, she begins to tell me of old hurts coming back. Or was it that she was trying to know if she could trust me to the end?

She brings back that moment in the car: I was driving, she was sick and sitting beside me. And then I understood she was telling me she thought or she feared that all along I've experienced her as a man.

All of our love life together, that was what I saw her as?

Never. Never. Never. I told her: Never.

Including sex, when she was fucking me? That moment—not that either, ever. Never.

I sat on the couch by her, and talked into her eyes. I said: "Remember when you first got sick, how I was getting reminded of my Pa sick at home so much, recovering from drinking binges? And I told you it's not you, it's just my memory from the past?"

I kept talking, I didn't know if she could hear me, she was so sick. The pain in my heart—twenty-two years and she doubted that I loved her for her complete self. I wrote a whole book about loving her because of her everything. And yet—

And I know, yes, I know, reader, that writing this now will never, never bring her back to answer my questions. I know that and yet I keep writing because I want her to answer, I want her to answer.

June 12, 2016

A friend sent me word that the Klan had littered a house in Birmingham with flyers that said "trans abomination," that said "go pee behind a tree." And when I looked, yes, there was the familiar graphic, the hooded man pointing a finger, saying "The Klan wants you"— to leave town, to die. Said they'd punish mixing Black with white, they'd punish mixing F with M, and any bi-going-in-between. No mixing, no mixing it up.

The power to put a symbol on anything, on a water fountain and say "white water" and "black water". Turn the four-pronged steel handle so the water spurts down like blood from a severed artery, spurts up in a sullied arc.

The national committee of one of the two ruling political parties in the U.S. is passing laws to make it illegal to walk through a toilet door if you don't match its little stick figure. Otherwise, they say, go outside into the woods, you belong outside "civilization," and pee behind a tree.

Or the police will come and drag you out before the world with your pants down and your cunt hanging out of your jeans or your balls hanging out of your dress.

The power to put a symbol on two doors, and say sheep that way, goats this way. One path to heaven, one path to hell. "Men" that way, "women" this way.

The power to use those words and deny there is any doubt, any doubt at all, about what the words mean.

The power to use those words to cut up your body, your dear, dear body. The power to press those words down over our lives, cutting a bleeding circle out of who we are. The punishment when you are someone who can go through either door.

The power to look at the two doors and to refuse to go through either. The power and the pride when you are someone who can go through either door, and do.

Now the anniversary of Stonewall, and the Tuscaloosa newspaper headline reads PRIDE. People are marching in New York City, San Francisco, Sao Paolo, Sydney—all around the world.

It's been two weeks, exactly, since the massacre at the Pulse gay dance club in Orlando, Florida. There 49 people—lovers, friends, mothers, children, many Latinx—lay dead and more gravely wounded.

So I saw the headline and foolishly thought, "Here's a bit of comfort, a word of courage." But no.

It was a brag about the Alabama football team, chosen by the editors for no particular reason this day except to scrape our raw wounds with the message that their PRIDE was not our queer PRIDE.

The first Pride event I went to wasn't in June. A man had been beaten to death on the Eno River, at a little swimming hole in North Carolina where gay men sometimes cruised. He was married, with two children, and then he was dead at the hands of those who hated queerness.

On April 17, 1981, over a hundred of us rallied in front of the Durham County Courthouse. Mab Segrest read a statement she'd written that began "We don't want to die."

That's pretty much the gist of why I ever march in Pride. That we still die dancing in a gay bar in Orlando because we are lesbian or gay or bisexual or trans, a relative or even a friend of queerness, proves the need to keep saying what should seem obvious: "We want to live." To insist that we have the right to live, dancing in the street.

Leslie and I marched once in Winston-Salem in the middle of lightning and thunder for North Carolina Pride. We held hands in the pouring rain, up to our thighs in the flood that swept past us in the streets. I was so happy. There was a time I had thought I might kill myself there, after I lost custody of the boys for my "crime against nature."

When she and I were marching, it was the mid-90s, Senator Jesse Helms was still doing his best to make our lives miserable, African-American churches were burning all across the South, and the Klan was having one of its revivals.

Leslie spoke of revolutionary communism and the crowd cheered. Hundreds of us chanted and sang and danced through the rain, shouting defiance.

At some point she let go of my hand and rushed away, to return with a present—a tiny plush trans-species bear sporting a pair of tie-on bunny ears.

My funny bunny, my Leslie, who knew so well how to live, who knew how to fight for our lives with every weapon she had, including laughter. Her smile, the dimple in her cheek when she smiled. Revolutionary optimism.

DAD IS PREGNANT

Jessica Dittmore

DOING IT BUTCH

reuben q.

exhibitionism at the grocery store when i hold their hand and cis men stare from across the aisle 'cause we do it better. hate gaze and fuck you too. you'll never be as real as me, a woman playing a man playing a woman, and i know i'm doing it right. it tastes like leather against skin against lips and steel toed, hot sweaty and tender doing pleasure all night. it smells like sweat from hard work scrubbing floors on your knees aching hands in the dirt making something new. never tell me how to love or live or feel 'cause i've dug my nails hard into living and hung on for dear life.

HOW CAN A WOMAN WHO IS WITH A TRANS MAN CALL HERSELF A LESBIAN?

Mary Vermillion

M aybe she wonders the same thing herself.
Maybe she wants to drive that question right out of her head. Because maybe, some twenty years ago, back when she was forty, that question almost caused her to leave the love of her life.

Maybe the love of her life, the trans man she is with—once a seeming lesbian, now her husband, always her beloved, her person, her one—maybe he doesn't stake his identity on hers.

Maybe, one Valentine's Day, some twenty years ago, he gave her a card that said *Whatever and whoever you would be without me, that is what and who you are with me. I cannot define who you are; our relationship cannot define who you are. Only you can define who you are.*

Maybe she had trouble defining who she was long before she met him.

Maybe when she was a little girl, she wondered why all the Disney movies had to end with a handsome prince instead of two beautiful princesses together. Maybe because she was born into a conservative Catholic family in a small Iowa town, she kept this question to herself. Because maybe even though she had never heard the word *taboo*, she understood it fully. Maybe before she started kindergarten.

Maybe when she was in junior high, she knew that she was a lot more interested in *Charlie's Angels* than most other girls. Maybe she also knew that most other girls were starting to get much more interested in boys than she was. Maybe she had a vague idea why, but she had a clear sense of what she should not say. Or think. Or feel.

Maybe when she was a freshman at Saint Mary, an all-women's college, she cuddled nearly every night with a senior. Maybe this senior, bold as she was, did not call herself a lesbian. Maybe none of the women there did.

Maybe it wasn't until she was in grad school that she met women who happily and proudly called themselves lesbian. But maybe by then, she was in a relationship with a guy. A 'cisgender' guy, although back then, no one knew the word 'cisgender'. Maybe her parents pressured them to marry.

Maybe the cisgender guy pressured her to stay married. Maybe he called her a bisexual.

Maybe she called herself a lesbian, and she divorced him.

Maybe before the divorce, but during the separation, the word 'lesbian' fueled her as she kissed a woman for the first time, made love with a woman for the first time. Made sense of herself for the first time.

Maybe by the time she left this woman and met her beloved—her person, her one—maybe she cherished her lesbian identity as if it were a Patronus straight out of *Harry Potter*. (This was long before JK Rowling shared her anti-trans views.) Maybe when she (our heroine, not Rowling) would summon her Lesbian Identity Patronus, it appeared as a ghostly version of Harriet in *Dykes to Watch Out For*. A soft butch—curvy, capable, calm. Maybe the Lesbian Identity Patronus—AKA Harriet—filled our heroine with confidence and courage. Maybe she thought it protected her from all things patriarchal or otherwise dangerous and unpleasant.

Maybe five or six years later, when her beloved—her person, her one—started coming out as a trans man, she fell prey to the mistaken belief that she would need to forfeit her Lesbian Identity if she stayed with him. Maybe she thought that if she lost her Lesbian Identity, she would lose her whole self. Her magic. Maybe she almost left her beloved, her person, her one. Maybe she almost bailed on what has become thirty glorious and enchanting years together.

Maybe now, when she calls herself a lesbian, it means both more and less than it used to.

Maybe she still loves calling herself a lesbian.

Maybe she doesn't always call herself a lesbian. Maybe when she senses the presence of transphobes (those who deny the reality of her beloved, her one), maybe then she calls herself queer.

Maybe she sometimes calls herself queer in solidarity with her some of her students: trans, pan, demi, enby, ace.

Maybe she sometimes calls herself queer because she is tired of fretting about her identity and defending it, even to herself.

Maybe she likes the history and the sound of the word 'lesbian.' Maybe she likes imagining Sappho on the isle of Lesbos, lyre in hand, surrounded by enthralled women, gently arcing palm trees, the ocean lapping the shore.

Maybe she loves her own history, the memories that live between her ears, between her years.

Maybe she treasures the first time she saw two women kissing each other on TV. 1991. She was in grad school, dog-sitting for a professor. It was *LA Law*. CJ and Abby. She called a friend (*Oh my God did you see it? Did you see it? Can you even believe it?*). Now she jokingly calls this friend her lesbian mentor, a volleyball teammate who showed her how lesbians can dance together and introduced her to the brilliant, charming human who would become her beloved, her person, her one.

Maybe her memories will not allow her to take lesbian representation for granted.

Maybe she still hungers for glimpses of women like herself. Women joyfully partnered with trans men, still calling themselves lesbians.

Maybe she wants to offer these women some company. Maybe she wants to feed her own belief that they exist. She does not want to hurt or offend the men they are with. She does not want to hurt any trans people. Or anyone in the LGBTQ+ community. But maybe she still sometimes needs to speak her truth.

So maybe that is how a woman who is with a trans man can call herself a lesbian.

SLOW DANCE

Taylar Christianson

after Merril Mushroom, Gabrielle Calvocoressi, Eileen Myles

The Slow Dance was very frequently done in the 50s. Be sure to begin with a general foxtrot-type step and don't hold your partner too close unless they seem receptive. If you don't know many fancy dance steps, you can do a simple two-step. Samovar, I said, sounds like a knight. It's just a fancy teapot. Lead with your right hand behind their back while they hold you around the neck with their left hand. Wrap the xeroform in broad yellow strokes and wind gauze around their fingers, like so. You can begin dancing by holding hands on the other side (your left, their right), but if they are receptive, you can ease your hands closer to your bodies until you manage to move your left hand around their waist. Drop coins between the tin lovers rattling loud mirror to mirror and wait for nothing to happen. If they move with you, you might want to breathe slightly on their neck. [ ]'s my samovar, the steam that makes my cheeks glow so all the women talk. If you can do fancy steps and they follow well, you can use whirls and dips as a good excuse to hold them tighter. This is a good way to impress both them and onlookers, but be very careful not to get out of control through showing off and stumble, fall, or—worst of all—drop them. My dear the back-pack you gave me has started to rip. Drive that white-star painted truck up here and come get your clay cat, your cardboard sword, your envelopes and cartoon gravestones and cereal box hats and when you're done throw me in the truck too and take me home.

TV-WSNO ON MUTE AT THE DYKE BAR IN THE SKY

Taylar Christianson

Suppose it's easy to slip
    into slacks fastened flat at the
    hips hook our keys to the belt loop where
your ripped-out fingers fit, scarred over white under
        short blood nails. I have, before, been tricked
    into doubting I have something worth
     watching, doubting floorboards will hold the square toes of
      dress shoes, goodwill cherries, green beetleshell boots
      under lace,
shirtsleeves dustblue on pitch red
        wood. Black me out with a hatchglass and paint me a
    bitch of a 'bird of a snow
       leopard—pin the pewter rose to my collar
       & kiss me before we step
     out. 1988 Pontiac Firebird, Trans AM, Miss Chatelaine,
        broadcast live
on fuzzy signal Snepsburgh WSNO above
           the bar. Swallowed by being seen.

SLOW AND WEIRD

Kimberly Dark

"Are you bisexual?" he asks me. Second date.

I shrug. "Sure." I hesitate, "though it's not really a word I use. I'm a femme dyke. I know that sounds out of fashion nowadays, but I'm old." I look at him with a half-smile, flirtatious. "Older than you. But bisexual, yeah, sure. Why do you ask?"

"All of the women I've really been involved with before have been bisexual." He says. We have already established that he's a trans man. Six years. He/him. Non-op. He is thirteen years younger than I, and looks something like some of the butch dykes I've dated. I enjoy the symmetry of the last person I dated having been thirteen years older than I. Older lovers are more my norm, but being 55 narrows the pool in that direction. Thirteen, the elder, also identifies as a trans man, but doesn't use male pronouns, prefers to avoid them entirely. Also non-op. Also not from my nation: USA. At the time she grew up and lived in Chile, gender transition was illegal. My current sweetie, thirteen, the younger, is Bulgarian and gender transition is still illegal. People buy hormones from Greece, administer them at home. No way to change documents, ever.

Thirteen the elder is history. It's the Bulgarian boyfriend who has hijacked my heart.

On our second date, I invite him back to my hotel room to smoke the joint he offered, but not to have sex.

"When then?" he asks earnestly.

"Third date," I say, with a coquettish tilt of my head.

"By the third date, most of my relationships are finished!" he laughs in frustration.

"Maybe this one will last a little longer," I say with a smile and though he's the one who blushes, I feel my skin temperature increase.

I texted on the day of date three, plans in place for later, still hedging, apparently. But not much. "At risk of making you blush again by talking about the sex we may or may not have . . . I am interested to know more about how you relate to your male body. Most pre- /non-transition people have 'no fly zones' or things they always or never do in bed. I mean, I suppose that's true of most humans really. Will you tell me some of yours?"

"No 'no fly zones' for me haha, although some things I would tell you if we got there. I am somehow super open in the bedroom, and everything flies hahaha . . . thanks for asking." His reply thrills me, and he tells me later that he doesn't usually bring the strap-on for the first time with someone. We are both pleased that he did with me.

"Why not?" I ask, slightly incredulous.

"A lot of women don't like it." He says.

I know this is true, of course, and I always feel badly for straight women who don't, because straight people act like they can't even have sex without a dick involved. But yeah, first time. It's polite not to make assumptions, and he is traveling across town to meet me. I'm glad he made a choice that suits us both.

"Either they don't like it, or they like it slow and weird somehow. Somehow that I don't really understand." He adds nuance to his first statement.

I laugh and repeat "slow and weird." I immediately recall a past lover with whom I had a pre-contact conversation in which she assured me that she intended to strap one on, but then went on to clarify, to my dismay, that wearing one didn't mean she had to use it "like a man." By which she clarified for my wrinkled brow, "You know, banging away like your feelings don't matter." She paused. "I know how to be slow and gentle with it too."

"And is that what you like when you're wearing the strap-on? Slow and gentle?"

"Well . . . " she raised her eyebrows looking for honesty and prudence.

"Yeah, me neither." I said. "Aren't you in luck."

Indeed, we were both in luck. Again, with the Bulgarian, I found myself extra lucky, and without as much discussion.

But let's be clear, I love the discussion too. Preferably while we're congratulating ourselves, after the sex, about how magnificent we are. I love the discussion, because we are navigating the changes that take place within us, and socially too. As we construct gender, we re-construct sex, which re-constructs gender. Of course, the two can exist independently, but for those of us who live outside both binaries of gender and sexual orientation—and still want sex—they are co-constituting. We are sliding along multiple trajectories with no constant angles. This is a 3d stream graph, and if we do it well, we enjoy each other's co-variants with zeal. We are co-constructing intimacies, alliances and intersections, while pleasure remains (at least relatively) constant. And maybe not at first, but eventually, and in community, these constructions have political consequences as well. That's the part that's exceptionally slow and weird—even when the fucking itself is exceptional.

I don't mind the word "bisexual" but it's somehow not political enough for me. And I'm old enough that "femme dyke" means something to me about my own intentionality of gender and sexual orientation. At my age, I feel the desire to insert, rather forcefully, that I am not a trans-exclusionary sort of lesbian. (I cannot even call this radical feminism, because the definition is incorrect, and it offends me to cede that term.) Sex is important to me, and so are the humans with whom I have sex, whether they call themselves trans men or women, or cis-men or lesbians or androgynous or non-binary. Some of these are a matter of time and place anyway. Sadly, I do know some who like a good rogering in bed, but still won't name and protect the people and desires they love. Queer folks can be homophobic too and misogynist. I recall learning that the woman who organized the Butch/Femme social group I sometimes attended was disgusted by the idea of butch/butch pairings. Too homo for her, it seemed. Whereas butch/femme was straight attraction, I suppose. I'd never seen it that way before, but it depends in part on how you come to what you do, how you feel, and who you do it with.

I think about Billy Tipton's wife a lot in this regard. He was a jazz musician, discovered to have female anatomy only by the EMT who tried to save his life. Suddenly the family was thrust into the public eye. His three adult sons didn't know he was assigned female at birth, but odder still, his wife didn't know. That's what she said and still insists. Let me pretend to understand her though. She had been a stripper, "the Irish Venus," before marrying Tipton and theirs seemed to be a very traditional marriage. To my mind, it's more likely they had a vibrant sex life, and as an experienced keeper of men's secrets—a woman who knew not to register acknowledgment of her best tippers in the park with their wives on a Saturday—she chose the narrative on which she and her husband had agreed. More important that they not seem queer, that she not be cast as a lesbian; I imagine they decided on the narrative that she just didn't know.

Of course, I can't know for sure and try to take people at their word. But I think about her. Straight women with trans men are probably different in many ways than lesbians with trans men. But maybe not all the ways. In my case, my queerness transcends sexual orientation (I am indeed now a woman, with a man) but maybe queerness can also be subverted by sexual orientation too, too impossible to admit. Are these personal or social relationships? Yes, I imagine they are, slow and weird.

I also consider the ways in which my lover and I have commonalities in our bodies—political ones, where our bodies have been objectified by the external gaze. Trans bodies and fat bodies have been made simultaneously hyper-sexualized and de-sexualized. Who would want the "ugly woman" or the fat woman? My identity as a fat femme dyke is another bridge to understanding my lover's experience. He is also stepping onto this bridge to my experience for the first time in his life. I am his first fat lover. The messages from broader culture are clear upon us though: my excesses and his conjuring of genitals and gender must make us nymphos.

The bridge between our experiences broadens in the places where the differences between us evaporate in others eyes. We are suspended through the act of erotic tension/difference.

Trans is increasingly seen as multi-directional these days. One to the other is not the only trajectory, even for trans men who generally pass well as cis men, especially with femmes beside them. The ability to consider and change, rather than rendering any choice static serves all of us in these aging, temporarily abled bodies. Regardless of gender, regardless of body shape and size. Consider boobs, which most trans men wish to divorce. My lover's ability to love my boobs but hate his own is political. I love the path my lover's on to release hatred for any part of the body-given. The boobs did nothing wrong, but they impede passing as male. They are unmanly for this reason. Rendering them invisible makes sense for men to soothe the wound of the external gaze—whether they are cis or trans.

My boobs too, however, are not acceptable as they are. As a post-menopausal woman with a D cup size, lack of a foundation garment would bring severe social stigma upon me in my culture (and most others). A brassiere with a proper shape allows me privilege. Our bodies are stigmatized and legitimized in different ways. As it stands now, boobs (properly arranged) are good for my social standing, bad for his.

What if a man's enjoyment of his own fleshy breasts (if he has them—cis, or trans) could be unfettered by the external gaze? What if it could be a personal matter, a matter between the man and his lovers, the man and his children. Would men lactate again more often? Most humans are biologically capable. Whether constricted by a binder or social prescription, the body can be a series of choices, a matter of allowing, a deep enjoyment and a disappointment all at once.

There have always been trans folks. It's not like those politicians who want to police restrooms don't know. People still feel entitled to dissect and make spectacle. Entitled to punish. Some of those people are lesbians. Some are trans themselves (the one with the biggest platform so far is Caitlyn Jenner). We are each capable of denying what we know, even when it arises in our own desires, our own experiences. Back on that bridge between experiences of fat femmes and trans men, it's also clear that everyone's known hot fat babes. And still, they can deny fat women as attractive. I know how solid those boners are for my soft folds and fat ass, even though people can't always admit it in public.

Witnessing others perspectives, pains and grief brings not just learning, but empathy. The loosening of attachment about bodies holds so much promise. Language itself can lead to the tightening of categories too—if we use it without nuance and consideration. My lover and I make sense together—not because we are a man and a woman, but because of all the other context I've mentioned here—and more. Our attraction and affinity feels like an evolution for me. Rigid meaning doesn't thrill me; I have no sexual orientation to it. When I was younger, I more often pondered the slippage of terminology: how we can be oriented toward that which changes position without losing the internal compass of queerness. I wondered this about lesbian desires for trans men. I also feared loving someone whose body could change in ways that trigger me negatively with smells and other sensory cues. Where are my triggers for desire? In me, or in the other? I'm more open to the mystery than I once was.

A category like femme dyke also makes me similar to other than lesbian in the way it brings political and cultural critique to class and appearance and conformity and acceptability. Doing it "like a man" connotes the disregard that men often feel for women and surely, that's social, not as often innate. Porn teaches us too, what our roles should be, but what happens when we uncouple from the roles. I think we've got a clearer chance of ending misogyny and enjoying human rights for all, if we own our urges. Our bodies show us what feels good when we can relax into them and not feel used. When we can relax into them and not feel we'll lose something if we don't use another. "Like a man" doesn't have to mean like an abuser. I definitely do not like the way cis men are socialized to use women, the ways in which we're not quite human to them. Insignificant. I am significant to my lover. He loves me. He adores my anatomy. We are in reciprocal discovery of our sex and gender and joy and becoming.

There's nothing slow and weird happening in our bedroom—at least not now. We are gusto and gustatory, eclectic and ecstatic. We manage joy and grief for the fact that our multiple abuses, and ways we have denied and returned to these bodies is both personal and social. But the work of repair we do is intimate. Repair and returning are iterative and the lit-up current to commit those acts crackles between us and sometimes arcs above us in inclusive ways I cannot comment on. Not just love—but the fucking too—can be bigger than just us. It is profoundly rooted and unhinged at the same time. By offering what words I can, I invite others to trace these metaphors back to their own actions, sensations and understanding. In what is gender and sex rooted and from what is it unhinged? The discussions are important too. I'm serious in the sentiment that we are helping to repair the world as well.

Knowing everything about identity and relationship is going to be slow and weird. And maybe impossible. How my queerness and his queerness coincide and co-construct can teach us things. We could both identify as straight now: one man, one woman. But we don't. On purpose. I cannot fathom claiming that terrain, thereby losing whole universes of hard-won possibility. A lot of things about gender and politics and pornography and consumerism and the external gaze are going to change slow and weird. But I'll still take fast and certain, at least one-on-one, whenever we can figure out how to make it.

GIRL COCK /
CONTRAPUNTAL FOR GIRL COCK

Zoe Cutler and Anne Haddox

I'm wordless with wonder,	I've evolved across time.
I see tits revealed,	my body has changed
then a dick,	leftover and emerging parts
laid on my bed like three joysticks,	combined into something mine.
And I am filled with joy;	I will not always celebrate.
as I cup her breasts,	today I protest,
said aloud: I love your strap.	I don't have the right parts.
she moans	awe, dismay, gratitude, disgust.

I use my form to please you.

A NAME LIKE CHOCOLATE, MELTING ON MY TONGUE

Suzanne DeWitt Hall

When I first met Declan, I was still a girl. Not by chronology, but by assignment at birth, inculturation, and self-identification.

We became acquainted in a conservative church, where I'd embraced the Christian concept of complementarianism and proselytized about the immutability of gender, warbling on about the thrusting nature of masculinity and the supple receptiveness of the feminine. I bought in completely to the mindset and all its virulent manifestations. My hair was long, my heels high, and makeup was a requirement before leaving the house.

Declan, by contrast, was never a girl, despite assignment at birth and insidious inculturation. But he wore bras he hated, gave up dreams of being a professional ball player, and did his best to cope with life while living it as someone he wasn't.

When we met, we were both married to men and proud of ourselves for performing the role of biblically-excellent wife despite Declan's gender identity and the turbulence and dysfunction in our marriages. We became good friends, close friends, deep friends.

And then we fell in love.

For as long as I can remember, my mother vehemently proclaimed that my name was *SUZANNE*. Not Sue, not Susie, not Susan. *SUZANNE*.

The etymology of Suzanne is "graceful lily": a soft and bending thing, implying fragrant fragility. I did my best to conform to that image.

We should be careful what we name things. Names have power.

Some years back, a client sang Leonard Cohen's *Suzanne* to me the first time we spoke on the phone. I'd never heard the song before, and his singing wasn't great. The experience was intensely uncomfortable. This was long before the #MeToo movement, and he was a client and a man, so I did what was expected and tittered in response, performing the role of bending lily according to the shape of my name and the generations of cultural expectations which traveled with it.

Rejection of all those expectations has been slow; the plates of my psycho-emotional terra shifting tectonically, unobservable without time-lapse image captures.

Suzanne.

I love reading old comb-bound cookbooks which include the names of the people who submitted recipes. In some of them, women list their husbands' names rather than their own, merely planting "Mrs." in front.

Mrs. Richard Dickinson.

Mrs. Franklin Würstchen.

Mrs. Peter Pene.

The identities of these women who lived, cooked, and loved has been erased, neither first nor surname printed as proof of existence outside of marriage. The rules of law and custom negated a need for individual identity, and being who and when they were, they bought into it, just as I bought into the concepts of gender fed to me in my own era.

Declan and I have been through several legal name changes together. First when we divorced our exes and took back our "maiden" names, then later, when we married. We each took the other's last name as a mutual giving and receiving of histories, of identity, of self.

Declan will soon change his first name from the one assigned by his parents to the one he chose. He likes the name on his birth certificate well enough when someone else bears it, but it was never him. When he pondered what his true name was, the sound arrived as epiphany, immediately resonating:

Declan.

Its truth settled around him, a mantle of affirmation and acknowledgment, a source of power and control.

Declan's mom struggles with this issue as many parents do. *Diane* was the name she selected at his birth, cooed as a young mother, and yelled as the parent of a teenager. It's the name she's always associated with the firstborn child she adores. Many parents feel like something is stolen from them if a name is rejected, as if the very act of naming gives them possession over our beings.

"Her name is *SUZANNE*," my mother demanded.

Possession starts with our parents, and for many women shifts to husbands who believe they possess us through the changing of our names. But no one possesses us, and possession doesn't equal love.

The importance of naming is a common theme in folklore and mythology. Jewish and Christian stories show characters being given new names at points of growth or change, connoting that the new name is a truer name. Genie lore instructs that knowledge of a person's true name gives you power over that person. A true name offers insight into their inherent nature, their essential being. Knowing it means knowing the person themselves. It means intimacy, and intimacy is power.

For years, I called my beloved *Dolce*; an Italian word which means sweet or dessert. The nickname was intimate and true in many ways; his presence was a gift, a reward for having choked down a lifetime of struggle which scoured my soul of pride and optimism. Declan was balm for that pain, tantalizing me with the taste of hope, of safety, of a future which promised comfort and delight. He made me realize that life could be delicious; a thing to be savored rather than an endless, painful cud-chewing.

Dolce.

My *Dolce.*

The word was like chocolate, melting on my tongue.

Writers tune in to the way letters combine or collide to create not only meaning, but sound and mouth feel. The D in

Dolce is harder than in *Declan*, but the rest is a soft trailing into the romantic. *Declan* is another experience altogether; the first syllable suggesting pine, water, and fresh air, the last syllable wrapping you in comfort and protection. Both names are lovely in their own ways, both contain Ds and Es and Cs and Ls, but they're so different in character. So particular in connotation and enunciation.

Transgender people understand the significance of names better than most. They endure an ongoing reality of being called something which is out of sync with their essential beings. The lucky ones, like Declan, get to explore what their true name feels like.

Declan was always *Declan*, regardless of what his parents called him. The name *Dolce* is still true and yet no longer fits him. He'll always be chocolate, but tempered, poured out, and molded into a shape of his ongoing making. He's himself now, even if his name doesn't conform to anyone's sense of ownership or of previous understanding.

Even mine.

When I was a teenager, I rebelled against my mother's insistence and asked people to call me *Zanne*. I liked the strength of the nickname. *Zanne* sounds like a superhero, whereas the soft susurration of the "suh" in front of "zanne" transforms it into lily-like submission. Decades later I abandoned *Zanne* when I left my ex-husband, because the power I'd felt in creating the sobriquet dissolved in the acidity of our marriage, eroded by the loudness of my insufficiency each time he spoke it. But I'm done defining myself by what others cling to or expect: a creature formed in their own image-making.

I'm ready to reclaim it:

Zanne.

Power is unleashed when we accept the truth of who we are and allow that truth to blossom and grow.

World-changing power.

Generational-trauma healing power.

Culture-shifting power.

As Declan explores the kind of man he wants to be, I'm invited to examine my own gender and name. *Suzanne* was my mother's demand. *Zanne!* became my exe's barked command. Now *I* get to choose who I am.

We all have the gift of crafting ourselves. And the responsibility.

Today my hair is short, my heels low, and makeup optional. I'm still figuring out what any of it represents. But I know one thing:

I want to be like Declan.

I want to be like chocolate, melting on his tongue.

FLOOR MAP 1979: RONALD/VERONICA'S BODY FALLING INTO GENDER AFFIRMATION SURGERY

Barbara McBane

From the rock that anchors Niagara Falls
Houdini falls.

Sounds of ankle bells shower in peals,
a cascade a cataract a stream of tears
hits the floor and resounds, a blow
to the saturated earth below.

That's their head

An abandoned mill-town huddles
and strings its crumbling factories
from former eras
along a tired river.

A rigid farmer and his upright wife
rake dark American furrows
in fields far away
from *des esperges*

of the French countrysides
over which Flora Tristan strides
on her way to the prisons in the colonies
to record their secret cruelties.

That's their torso

Water flows to the right
veers to the left
tumbles from the height
of a couch.

Isadora Duncan's
thin scarf

falls earthward,
choking back volumes.

Convictions in conflict—
thoughts scribbled on red cocktail napkins
where ink stains spread darkly like tears that tear
the thin crumpled substance.

That's their organs, heart

Ronald-Veronica as cyborg was
gestated, incubated from tattered
red napkins and out of
the blue vinyl seats in a diner:

drenched and dried out and hung
from a fluorescent grid overhead,
formica table, test tube, hospital bed.
Ronny-Veronica writes instead

in her journal, from a beige Hayward flat
strapped inside a prison of possibilities.
Ronald Friedman turns left
Veronica Friedman turns right

a red sedan hydroplanes
through the night
leaving nothing but skid marks
in the rearview mirror—

That's their legs

split truths harmonized
by the plague doctor
wearing his stiff white coat, his
black tie and plastic pocket

protector, with a pen in his right hand.
A pipe in his left

forms a checkmark—
ditto his mouth, its smirk.

Near the roadway, a child grips
a rusting gate tight in two fat fists
with its back—the butt of its gender—
aimed at our camera.

It peers into some kind of garden—
a luminous pastel pink and blue wash
whose precise contents
we're left to guess.

That's their appendix

The card displaying *this* image says
Outsider. We discover no legible emotion.
Lead-gray cirrus clouds itch, scratch,
drag over the horizon.

The gripped gate hangs
between stone walls.
What is this century?
Is it a cemetery?

That's their arms

Two stoned girls struggle
by the side of a highway, their angry words
lost in a traffic and truck storm:
a human-inhuman din.

Soft machine-body, two bodies in one
body of surgical intervention—
body of thought:
Ronald and Veronica:

That's their clasped hands

a convergence of ideas,
a divergence of forces.

A circle turns in on itself
like the curving horn of a goat
                              That's their tongue twisting

with its leg lifted to run.
A paper napkin flutters
down from the height of the falls:
a red fleck, a small prick

of inflammation, a dot in a massive
concatenation, a roaring
wall of water,
of sound.

Ronald or Veronica's dropped wet red glove
contains scribblings:
marks that form a trail of crumbs
through a fairy-tale forest

which a strange congregation—
stingray, platypus, mantis and squid—
have eaten. Ronny-Veronica
can't even *try* to go home.
                              That's their hands wringing
So, turning in on Veronica's hospital bed
we watch and spin. The delicate napkin
entombed in the archive box—
or the slipper or glove or hat in its hatbox—

are parts of a body of fashion—
or a fashion of bodies, draped, dropped, overturned
and falling.
The distance of history turns a tangled mass

of gendered body-parts into an infinite knot,
Houdini's body: contortable,

inescapable, ever in question.
Fantasies collide.

> *That's their head aching*

Flora Tristan slides
through the asylums of London,
the seaports of France, or through Paris, where
the same stone walls that divide

the streets support rusty gates in the countryside.
Alexandra Kollontai pours over her papers
in her poorly lit quarters before stepping out
on the stage of public political speaking

as—creaking—the door to her dark room swings open,
then shut and a bright light explodes,
and beyond is—*what?*
A blazing sky

> *That's their hand writing*

at 32,000 feet high.
Below, a soldier shoulders a gun,
barricades at the Commune—
1871

Parachute in place, Alexandra
(or Ronald/Veronica) creeps
toward an ultimate act of trust—
dropping into the glowing air that cuts—

> *That's their dream-life*

a twisting red streak through a white shine,
a flutter of color, scarf lifting with wind,
trailing out behind her front-facing gaze,
around, down

and stop. Sudden freeze of the wheel,
quick impact on receptive ground.

That's their fall from grace
Veronica slowly produces a very large napkin—
clean, soft—of cloth.

She puts it to use: to mop up and mend
the fallen or flying bodies with
their fought-over parts and clashing fashions
and throats that open break or bend.

maybe gross messes—either/or
radiating splatters and luscious patterns
of tissue, ink and blood on the boards
That's how they end their sentence

JENNIFER

Cupid Maville

TO BRING MORE JOY IN LIFE

Lily Kaylor Honoré

*O*ctober 2020. *Dear Grad School Classmates,*
     After reading the essay about nonbinary speakers of grammatically gendered languages and the linguistic strategies that they've created to better communicate their identities, our breakout Zoom group had a lively discussion. We spoke about the built-in power structure that languages encode and impose upon marginalized people, and some possible implications for future writing and translation, as languages continue to evolve. How might future translators of English, if the language eventually moves on entirely from "he" and "she," look back and translate those terms? I wondered if any fiction writers had explored worlds in which humans are not categorized by their genitalia. I mentioned a poetic question my mom posed, some years ago, when I explained to her my friend's use of "they," as a genderqueer/nonbinary/trans person. "Do they use the plural word because they contain both, both a male and a female self?" she mused. While possibly not the idea behind that pronoun's newer usage in English, and certainly not true for everyone who uses it, that did fit my friend beautifully. Less beautifully, being misgendered turned out to be a concern which outlasted them.

October 2020. Dear Professor,
     I should inform you that I'm dealing with a loss that is making it hard to concentrate on school. I really thought I was fine at the beginning of the semester, but either that was a tad optimistic, or a friend's mom's death brought it up again. I estimate I'm currently at about 25% brain power.

June 2020. Dear Poet,

It's quite lurid. My friend left me a phone message, so I knew that there was going to be a body, and I knew when, but I didn't know where. Cue the most ridiculous police involvement, such broad comedy that no one would believe me—and they didn't, I guess, which is why one cop in one part of San Francisco didn't bother to take down a report from me and never followed up, though it turned out my friend was already in the SF city morgue by then, identified, with a different cop trying to locate someone to notify. As I had to make 11 days worth of phone calls myself to find this out, I think our city detectives are not very good at detecting. For further burlesque humor, my friend, Alyx, a trans guy who identified as genderqueer and used they pronouns, possessed a California ID that said "male" and a body that, to some, still said "female." As I got very good at explaining briskly to receptionists searching databases for John and/or Jane Does.

June 2020. Dear Parent, Sibling, Sibling, Friend, Friend, & Friend,

Hello, my six closest people! (I'm in an accounting mood.) I had three friends left in San Francisco and now I am down to two. When I moved into this apartment, over twenty years ago, the neighborhood was aswirl with cute young artsy dykes. Just walking down the street was exciting, all of us in bloom together. Not so much anymore, in this now trendy corner of the Mission District. The wave of gentrification we accidentally ushered in— everyone knows it was the mostly-white broke artists and bohemian queers who made this mostly-Latino working-class area so palatable to the *new tech riche*—has swept all but a few of us away. So I am melancholy about this sudden 33 % reduction of intimates still in my area code.

It's funny: though I'm probably closer to any of you in some mathematical equation of blood, years of friendship, or recent hours hanging out, only Alyx

1. had met all of you, when not all of you have met each other
2. had met other people in my life, who some or all of you have never met, and
3. had heard a lot about all of you, though only some of you have heard a lot about Alyx.

October 2020. Dear Professor,
Five months ago a close friend of mine, a onetime roommate who I've tried to rescue many a time, died via suicide. We had known each other for nine years and had briefly dated. My friend struggled with addiction and depression and at the end of their life lived in a van that didn't run with no access to electricity or bathrooms once everything shut down for shelter-in-place. The gym they joined to take showers, the library where they could've charged their phone, and the mental health clinic where they might've refilled their meds, all closed their doors in March. My own door was closed to Alyx, too. I was too afraid: the new virus, spread through air, my friend's drug, inhaled in smoke, purchased only on the poorest, most crowded Tenderloin streets. They asked if I wanted to get together, a game of backgammon, and I said no. In a few weeks, I said, when the stay-at-home order ends. I didn't know that there would be no more time.

By the time the Medical Examiner's Office had decided that my friend's homophobic, transphobic Christian family really was not going to call back and assume responsibility for the body and that a friend could now step forward and take disposition of the remains, a month's worth of storage fees had piled up. Fees to pay to the City to get Alyx's body out of hock. Fees to pay to a funeral home, at a time when we couldn't gather for funerals. Fees we couldn't afford. We: me and those of Alyx's exes, dance party acquaintances, and old friends who could be found on Facebook. At exhaustive and exhausting length, we collectively decided to do nothing, to let the City treat Alyx as indigent. The tradeoff for allowing the City to absorb the expense—cremating and then anonymously scattering my friend's ashes in the Bay, batched in with this year's other unclaimed human remains—means that we forfeited the right to claim their journal, photo album, or whatever else was in the backpack I wasn't allowed to see, along with the body I wasn't allowed to visit.

June 2020. Dear Parent, Sibling, Sibling, Friend, Friend, & Friend,
I'll probably switch between they/he pronouns for Alyx. I knew them more recently as "they," but older friends of theirs still say "he" or "she," depending on how far back their Alyx vintage, and it's easier to say "he" to the coroner as that's the most recent legal designation. Alyx was interested to hear about the new nonbinary category for California ID's but hadn't done that yet.

Though we had very different ways of being in the world and different experiences of that world, there is another kind of commonality built from shared experiences. And living together in a studio apartment, one accrues (two accrue) a lot of shared experiences. Alyx lived with me on and off for three years, first in my bed, then renting the closet, finally on a mattress wedged half-under the kitchen table. Alyx probably overstated the case when, once, they introduced me to a date of theirs as their "platonic life partner." But despite his own problems—and despite an inauspicious beginning when he stood me up on our first date and despite some fucked-up things some of you know about but none of us shall talk about here—he cared about me a lot, during a period in which I'd needed a lot of caring.

They: tried to get me writing again and took me to a poetry group downtown. Tried to get me outside of my apartment, sitting on grass at local parks, rec centers, and median strips. Called a laundry service when that got too overwhelming. Took the bus with me to doctor's appointments when that got too overwhelming. Put together the easel that'd been in its box since 2006. Helped me staple blue sequined fabric to the ceiling. Looked through my art books and found a Man Ray photo to recreate with household objects, before that became a thing. Tried to find us both new friends by starting a friend meet-up group, before that became a thing. Tried to get me dates (there were four successes, however brief, with the butch women they pushed me towards at daytime queer dance clubs, and one failure, after much plotting, with a crush). Worried about my cardiovascular health when my weight went up and dragged me on fast walks up very long hills.

Through Alyx, I learned about Leigh Bowery, the Dipsea hiking trail in Marin, Lykke Li, Fever Ray, aquarium care, begonia care, what zombies were, that there were dirty videos viewable freely on the internet, how to drink sugared malt liquor beverages from paper bags, how to play backgammon according to more-fun made-up rules, how and why to give a cat children's benadryl, and that a chihuahua could actually be an okay dog.

Don't forget the fashion. Alyx styled me for the OKCupid photo shoot (cleavage, boots, gold lamé) and then OK'd my look for the first date (long black chiffon and sequin mesh) which netted me a lovely few years with my most recent girlfriend. Alyx shopped with me in the teen girls' section at Ross, dressed up with me in coordinating vintage to go to El Rio, wore my spandex leggings and never returned my pink baby tee. Convinced me to go in on a pair of rainbow and black platform boots in between our two shoe sizes. Painted our nails at the kitchen table, black glitter for them, teal glitter for me. Split packs of hair bleach and passed the clippers back and forth, touching up their short wavy crop/mohawk/buzz cut and my red/blue/blond/pink/short/long undercut. Mixed cocktails for the putting-on-makeup part of getting ready for clubs. I hadn't had a femmey friend in a while, and I really liked that they liked me to do their makeup. That this femmey friend was also both male-gendered, non-gendered, and a lesbian is one of the complexities of our modern era. Or, as Alyx had me write, in purple eyeliner pencil above the waistband of their hot pink hot pants, for the Trans March at Dolores Park: *Gender Schmender*.

February 2021. Dear Everybody,
Alyx made a lot of questionable decisions. Brave, but also impulsive, reckless. Pushed down by life, occasionally flaring into belligerence, but also meditatively quiet, calm-spoken. Green eyes sliding into topaz—they'd watched every nature documentary ever made. A Rooster Scorpio five years older than me, Alyx worried the testosterone injections which gave them a body they loved might also lead to them "losing my pretty." An atheist who instantaneously acquired a belief in afterlife after smoking DMT in my bathtub. They never once yelled at me, and I cannot say the same. So many tries at rehab. Phone calls they didn't remember, loans they didn't repay. Moving in with women and getting kicked out. Losing an Uber car to unpaid parking tickets. Finally making it to the top of a waitlist for supportive housing in a single room occupancy building, and then having to share a toilet with a man who left shit on the seat. By then, having given away most of their possessions in prior suicide attempts, Alyx let his hair grow in dark, stopped wearing colors. In the SRO and surrounding SOMA streets, for safety, they dialed down their genderfabulousness, and just passed as male, hoping not to be outed as FTM. Despite chronic pain and the foot surgery and the back surgery and the bike accident and the shoulder surgery, Alyx kept on working, zipping takeout to app users on an hourly-rental stand-up scooter. A hotel clerk job was easier on the body but workplace restrooms were a problem. Once the case with the City finally settled, the accident which left them with a metal plate in their shoulder ("I'm bionic") with what was left after the personal injury lawyer's cut and after the high-interest cash advances from that lawyer, Alyx moved out of the SRO and into the blue van. It stopped running the next week.

October 2020. Dear Anybody,
Today is Alyx's birthday. I dressed up in rather elegant gothy black and put on jewelry with my surgical mask to walk to the

liquor store on the corner. I bought a candle and two chocolate-flavored BuzzBallz. "My friend used to get these here," I told the man at the register, "My friend who died. Alyx. Blond? Kind of short?"—I indicated with my hand—"Cocky little shit." My voice wavered on the last word. The shopkeeper politely pretended to remember.

February 2021. Dear Alyx,
I love you. I miss you. Thank you. I'm sorry. I'm trying.

June 2020. Dear All My Remaining Loved Ones,
One year for Alyx's birthday we took the cheap bus to Reno, just the two of us, and Alyx turned twenty bucks at the nickel slots into first one hundred and then zero dollars, finding both directions equally enjoyable, and got in trouble for climbing onto a faux-marble fountain faun. I took a picture as we rode down a mirrored escalator, infinite Alyxes looking back at me. They are smiling, arms crossed over an unseasonable white undershirt, brightly colored tattoos spreading down their arms and back. Both sunglasses and readers are pushed up on their bleach-blond head. The tiniest, tenderest bit of receding hairline. Goatee stubble smudged over dimpled chin, one tadpole-plucked eyebrow quirked.

October 2019, their 50th and final birthday, we walked through an SF Open Studios warehouse where they greeted by name a homeless older gentleman in a natty suit, ate too many lavender-hibiscus donuts, unknowingly upset me by touching a painting's textured surface, stood on a chair to help an older lady straighten something crooked, requested my help enrolling in a future City College course, and wrote down in a photographer's notebook a childhood-memory essay on the prompt of Barbies and gender. I'd made a card writing out their strengths and my future hopes for them and brought roses. I was the only person who marked their 50th birthday at all.

Their official date of death is May 11th, 2020, the day they were found in a hotel on 6th Street. The call I missed with their goodbye message was from the 9th. Their phone rang until the 12th. It was the 14th when my friends went looking for the van, the 15th when I told the police there might be a body in that van, the 20th when I alerted their old friend and their ex, the 21st when I called the ER, and the 22nd when I called the morgue. As I brightly said, "My friend is missing, and I thought I should check to see if he is with you." And they were.

February 2021. Dear World,
The last time I saw Alyx Francisco was February 8th, 2020. I accepted their last-minute invitation to hear a DJ set at the Midway, the Desert Dwellers. As we were leaving my apartment, zipping jackets to head to the bus stop, Alyx called me into the kitchen. They pointed up above the window, near the ceiling. Years ago, I had climbed up on the kitchen table to write on the wall, in twelve-inch red lipstick letters: *To Bring More Joy In Life.*

"I always liked that," Alyx said. They picked up their backpack. "I always tried to be that."

A FORCE TO RECKON WITH

Deanna Armenti

for the Love of my life

Your body is a shrine
to your spirit.
A living document
of who you are.

One that you have
written on and carved into
lovingly, knowingly.

You handpicked your name
and gave it to yourself,
like choosing the perfect wildflower
from a field of prospects.

Your chosen scars
are power,
reshaping what was into what is
and what has *always* been
your truest self.

You handed yourself liquid conviction,
assurance in the shape of T.
A green Band-Aid in one hand
and a needle in the other,
you are a force to reckon with—a hurricane lives within you.

I WAS ONCE A FEMME:
IDENTITY THEN AND NOW
Urszula Dawkins with Alex Nichols

Butch-femme in the Nineties/Noughties

Waiting for her drink, she runs a broad hand over her scalp—leans over to hide her breasts. Thighs heavy inside her pants, big and tactile. Oblivious to me, but how could she be? Because I've done it before, walked past her with the look of acknowledgment that doubles as a careful look away. She stands defiant, silent, vulnerable, proud. Doesn't see the compromise in my posture, the way my decadent body leans towards her from across a room. I smell the femaleness inside her clothes. Beneath her lowered voice. Behind the body language. Inside her hands, driving their sensitivity.

Leaning against her car with our groins together, heaving. I reach round the back of her waist to feel its thickness. Fleshy and womanly even in its hardness and strength. The base of the spine, the small of her back. Want to feel her weight on me. She runs her hand down the front of my neck and keeps it against my throat. I know she is feeling her power and my response to her. For the flesh of the throat is full of sensors. It knows the danger and eroticism of that touch, the hand of another in that vulnerable place. It is the body releasing a memory of life and death when the butch places her hand against my throat.

Coming out in my thirties felt like starting all over again. Relating intimately to women was a mystery, and it was as if I'd thrown a chunk of myself out—all the experience of the tensile dance of "woman" and "man." I was a dyke, feeling proud, excited, but over time something seemed erased, lost. Then I discovered Joan Nestle, both her writing and her person, as she moved to Melbourne and began to appear at events, erotic readings, talks. *A Restricted Country*[1] and *The Persistent Desire*[2] opened up a world to me where I could queerly name my desire line: femme-butch. It drew me a map of the relation-in-difference that fuels me erotically. My queerness wants tension. The tension produces questions about "self" and "other." Not having the answers is sexy.

"The butch always cooks," said a friend, flummoxing me. But *yes*. This new relation was not fixing-the-car versus lipstick-and-heels. Not heteronormative and not normative-masc versus normative-fem. I love the press of cleavage against shirt, but the butch is not a man. I'm protective of her. She protects me. We are different in our bearing, in our styles of care. She indeed cooked—the butches so often cooked and better than me. She is more vulnerable than me. I pass. She doesn't. We don't understand the other's position. Not really. Yet we fit. Deliciously.

The butch quakes in her boots at the first touch of a woman's hand. A femme has her power, and knows almost certainly that the butch will find a way to thwart it. Perhaps before the courtship is sealed, but maybe not. For years she may engage in the dance with her butch lover and be cared for like never before. But caught up in the seduction of difference, the butch struggles to evade her clutches: the beautiful chthonic must be kept at bay. The femme can never allay that fear. For there is indeed everything to lose in the erratic mire of the woman.

---

1 Joan Nestle, *A Restricted Country: Essays and Short Stories* (London: Sheba Feminist Publishers, 1988). **Editor's Note**: Selections from *A Restricted Country* appear in *Sinister Wisdom*'s **Sapphic Classic** of Nestle's work, *A Sturdy Yes of a People* (2022).

2 Joan Nestle (ed.), *The Persistent Desire: A Femme-Butch Reader* (Boston: Alyson Publications, 1992).

When I feel her eyes upon me and know that I play havoc, it is a delicate triumph of intersecting gazes. I know she sees my power. When she tells me her deepest feelings or sheds her tear against my skin, I'm flooded. I've got her, and if she curls into me and her breath deepens—ah yes, her tear wets the gentle space between duct and ear where expression does not travel. [3]

There is a fatalism in this early writing (c. 1996–2002), as much as it is loaded with pleasure and desire and as much as it honors the power and wonder of the "masculine woman." This writing both celebrates and interrogates the tension of butch-femme, an exquisite (pleasurable + painful + bittersweet) binary—a dance perhaps ritualized, there being "rules of play," however movable or loose. Femme gave me a sense of continuance as a person as I left heterosexuality behind. That decade or so of femme enabled me to bring my intimate history, with its interplay of differences, into the lesbian space.

Field work: identity shifts in faraway places
More than a decade after completing the body of work called *What She Wants*,[4] and now in my fifties, I was alone. I stayed alone and became lonely. I created romances for myself by traveling, lucky (and privileged) enough to secure occasional writing residencies. One time I found myself in a high-Arctic mining town, my queer identity rendered invisible by layers of polar fleece and nobody knowing me. But even in that place, I could spot a butch at 100 yards.

In the story I wrote, the butch and the femme encounter one another repeatedly—not in a sticky bar-room, but on the tundra of the Nordic outback—without ever properly meeting.

---

3 Adapted from notes on butch-femme, circa 2002.

4 *What She Wants* encompasses a series of queer, erotically charged stories published in various anthologies, a book-length unpublished manuscript and a limited-edition artists book (2014).

As I round a bend in the path, we come face to face. There is no more ignoring me here: we say good day to one other and briefly speak. She comments on the weather, on the view back towards the mine—things anyone might exchange with a stranger—and nothing in her words betrays her. She is utterly clear to me, and I to her, but the elision is absolute: boots over wet rock could not slip more easily.

I want to touch her, simply to reach in and shatter the thing that closes both of us. What is her skin like, what secrets would come from her mouth if there were no more guardedness? She is consummate at deflection, and I am so good at pointing away to the landscape, to anything that isn't me.

What would I do if you came to me, finally? It would be as terrifying as leaving the town and walking into the wilderness; as terrifying, equally, as losing myself in the black rock tunnels, placing my hands on their cool walls. If you are 'other' to me, it is because you mirror: a dark glass that ultimately shows the same self-protection, the same subtleties of retreat and hunger and survival and passion, from the other side of that reflective plate.[5]

In the isolation of this story, femme and butch come together in a relation where they no longer play opposites but each remain self-protectively distant. It's no longer a dance but a stand-off. The pleasure is still there, counterintuitively—*knotted up* and with no chance of unravelling. But also, the writer is queerer now, and much, much further away in time from the masc/fem dynamic and history that butch-femme helped honor throughout and beyond the first years of "dykedom."

---

5 Adapted from Urszula Dawkins, "Field Work, Prospekt: Butch-Femme in the High Arctic," *Writing from Below* 3 no. 1 (2016), https://writingfrombelow.org/masc/field-work-prospekt-femme-butch-in-the-arctic-landscape/

Falling for Alex: a fresh insistence

From 2017, life takes a significant turn. I begin to correspond, converse and court with Alex, who is trans. One of our conversations is about *insisting* on my queer and thus "incoherent" place in a normative, "coherent" world that increasingly denies me, the older "woman." (I am starting to be unsure what "woman" means.) I'm trying to articulate something new about identity. I journal a lot:

> *Our* insistence *is the creation of a way of being that seduces the world into not denying us and that allows or enables us to be a socially operating part of it. It is our ability to charm, to make the normative other feel they are safe, to make ourselves irresistible, in a way.*
>
> *It is equally and also a political position, a queer position, and a position that spells recuperation, not insanity. On the side of sociality, there is insistence on existing, of being 'part of'. And on the side of the self, and the intimately relational self, there is the insistence that that incoherent space is not a space of dysfunction or arrested development but rather of life, creativity and eroticism. It is the chthonic source of all the passion that feeds all the desire and transformation and change in the world. In a sense, it is the ultimate, swirling optimism, imaginative, full of potential.*[6]

Alex says to me, "I want to get you to let go of your interest in the self, because I think there are other really interesting things you could turn your mind to."[7] This, and the confidence with which they say it, is deeply sexy to me—that they should show themselves with such surety, and that they should propose to change me. They tell me:

---

6 Journal excerpt, 2017.

7 Email from Alex, 2017.

The self is like gender: a necessary fiction . . . We live in and through it; perhaps we cannot be without it, not in the form the social currently takes it.[8]

Gender, they suggest, is continually formed and re-formed through interaction. They ask me to think about the self the same way—as a non-thing made of the web of contingencies, relations, that can be seen as both constituting it and being constituted in turn.

A turn indeed. What a dance.

We sit on a concrete bollard, and it is as bright as a photograph, the car park behind and the density of the ocean before us. You are right next to me, except that there comes a time when you lean away and I wonder why, what feeling is so profound in your body, that you do not press near. I do not try to be closer; there is something in me that is so full of you and yet can leave you separate. I don't know how I do it, for my passion at this point is dizzying.

The lights in the channel signal their message, which we don't understand. You talk about the sea, about being in it, diving under it, and I say I'm afraid of being under it. But in saying it, I want to no longer be afraid, I want you to show me, I want you in the darkness to change me.

On my hand next morning I write, "nonsovereign."[9]

Being with Alex brings an unexpected shift. My gender is caught in the headlights now—what actually is it?

Alex:

That's my recurrent question, and the image of the headlights catches something of the sharpness with which

---

8   Email from Alex, 2017.

9   Journal excerpt, 2017.

I project it outwards at others. "What is it?" was a question stage-whispered by my peers on the school bus as they looked me up and down. But this romance has felt like a coming home—the glamour and care of the femme holds a space in which I can extend into who I might be. This is the first relationship in which I feel free enough to call myself "they." I can inhabit the position of (masculinized) complement without having to be a "he."[10]

I drop my defenses, and femme in many ways drops away along with them. Now I feel queer and somewhat genderqueer, with femme interludes. The genderqueerness might be readable if I were 25. But I'm 63, and no-one polices my gender—age desexualizes and thus degenders me in the eyes of the world. Now I am less fixated on the dyadic, intimate relation and more concerned with where I—and we—can fit (differently, mutually) in relation to the world. Alex again:

But to me, your sexiness starts with femme. Looking at the curves of your hips, belly and breasts, I feel a self coalesce around desire for this differently gendered other. Yet the caress, like our words, moves us away from this dyad. Both are reflexive and begin to dissolve the clear-cut edges of "I" and "you." So too the (liberatory) promise of romance is suspended, for there is no single arc or destination.[11]

We use the word "shimmer" for these moments of potentiality and uncertainty.

Roland Barthes writes of an "inventory of shimmers, of nuances, of states, of changes (pathè)" as they gather into "affectivity, sensibility, sentiment" and come to serve as "the passion for

---

10 Alex Nichols, notes for this article.

11 Alex Nichols, notes for this article.

difference."[12] For us, "shimmer" describes the slightest feeling and the ongoing process by which these states arise and change, and points to how the one experiencing this affect is emerging and shifting in relation—to both the feelings and the world.

Shimmervoyage: A Queer Spec-fic

I have no trans experience—none of the pain of not fitting gender assigned at birth. But somehow my gender—or really, the acts of societal refusal I have made and the ways of thinking that are queer and non-normative (unwomanly)—aligns painfully with an ever-starker disconnect from my family of origin, an alienation that I've begun to realize is deep and scarring.

I start writing anew, inventing a world where there is no day/night distinction but instead a permanent twilight. Here there is no gender—the humanoid inhabitants are the asexual larvae of a mysterious species that inhabits (and procreates in) the skies. In this world lives Sanze, of the Lēvv.

Sanze's pronouns ē, ēh, ēm are derived from ēh place of hatching and confer ēh societal position as well as many obligations and expectations. These pronouns are not gendered: only after cocooning and then "flying" will there be "male and feme." But Sanze's people, the ev, still couple in romantic monogamy—"onelove"—and imagine a male/feme reunion after metamorphosis.

"It's beautiful, isn't it?"

Sanze glances up at the speaker to see two dark eyes watching ēh before flicking back to ēh hand. Ē's been trying on the worked gold bands from the market stall and hasn't seen the stranger step up beside ēm.

"See this little twist in the filigree? It's the maker's signature, I bet."

---

12 Barthes cited in Melissa Gregg & Gregory J. Seigworth (eds), *The Affect Theory Reader* (Durham & London: Duke University Press, 2010), 11.

Ē is abashed and drawn in. Annoyed at what seems a kind of arrogance. But those eyes.

"I've offended you. I'm sorry."

"I haven't seen you before. I'm Sanze, of the Lēvv—but I left Lēvv as soon as I could."

"Rish," a hand extends towards ēh.

"Of . . . ?"

"Just Rish."

Limini? thinks Sanze. Ē feels ēh cilia jitter against ēh chest.

"You think I'm showing off," Rish continues, "but I just love these small treasures. I forget myself."

There's a pause. Then the goldseller, who has been gossiping with a neighbor, coughs sharply. Sanze still holds the ring, and the two are blocking the boardwalk. Ē puts it down abruptly. Blushes and steps away with no idea where to go.

"I'm intruding."

"No!" The blush deepens.

There's a commotion behind them—shoppers dispersing, sellers hastily pulling their wares in—uniforms, people running. Bolting. Oh no. Recruiters, out to press-gang limini. Ē grabs for Rish's hand to pull them away but feels a strong grip and counter-pull.

"Better to hide in plain sight," Rish says quietly.

Of course. Rish is passing. No need to run. So it's true. They're limini.[13]

Within Sanze's world, the *limini* are those who do not invest in onelove nor the notion of reuniting with their lover in the skies. They pair, not always monogamously, but to limini, love encompasses all beings. They call it allo, a contraction of "all-

---

13 *Shimmervoyage*, the Alaïde chapter. Work in progress.

love." Born among the ev, limini do not "come out" but "step away," rejecting ev obligations altogether. Because they refuse all traditional allegiances, they lose their pronouns and are referred to only as *them*, thus othered. They are persecuted in ways both subtle and overt.

The limini have something Sanze longs for and will come to witness—the allo that makes and is made by close community, collective care, and a connecting ethic that eclipses onelove. But to give up your pronoun is to lose your belonging and to embrace a life of alienation and risk.

The inspiration for the limini is my trans partner's close networks, in which I see a care and holding of one another like nothing I have witnessed before. It is built—like the historical butch-femme dyad—from the learnings of oppression, and the view from the outside is inevitably both rose-colored and obscured.

In Sanze's relationship with Rish, the pleasurable fatalism of a dance of opposites is replaced with a back-and-forth shuffle between a certain queerness in Sanze and the absolute queerness of the limini. Theirs is an uncomfortable alliance across cultures, political differences, ethics and beingness in the world. Of course, it's an allegory of the cis/trans binary, an attempt to question what that boundary exactly is and how it can be navigated—whether and where belonging can exist.

But what of intimacy in this world of outlaws and allies, where there is no "sex" as such, but bodies still come close?

The two are silent now, watching the movement of light on the ceiling—passing vehs, flashing signs. Finally, they turn towards one another.

Rish's cilia are long, some turning blue among the coal-black, stirring in controlled waves that pass from armpit to collarbone to ribs in a dance that tastes in Sanze's mouth like plum and stream water. Ēh own cilia strain in response and a blush covers ēh torso. Rish embraces Sanze and draws ēh closer. Ē touches Rish's back, in wonder at the velvety interlock of diamond-shaped scales, their cool-warm breathing supplementing Rish's already shallowed nosebreath.

They're sinking; spines are moving in tiny increments in a space that gets stiller and stiller, even the breath an ecstasy of silent, slowing air, until only the scales draw in oxygen. Their eye movements slow, enter a mirror phase and then cease. Sanze's hips are jelly, throbbing. The only movement now is magnetic, as the cilia find one another and touch in pulses of pale light. The lovers' irises are fixed wide. They remain like this as the caress of shared energies—kesh for inner life and kékesh for connectedness—continues. Neither can move. Time has slid away into the gaps between fingers, ciliatips, skins.[14]

Of this scene Alex writes:

This is difference unmoored from the boring dyad of "man" and "woman," though still with sensuous and erotic investment through some of the luscious tropes of femininity and masculinity—cilia and spines are like fingers and cocks; scales are velvety like vulva. But these new (alien) surfaces and organs—with their trembling, blushing, straining, stirring, throbbing—could be any and no gender. They mark out new terrains for the eroticized body; they give a language for our trans/queer sex.

Rish sees Sanze differently from how ē sees ēmself. I do not think of my lover as cis, for she is not defended and defending against the uncertainty and ambiguity that trans holds open space for. Rather, she is with me in the unfolding

---

14 Shimmervoyage, the Alaïde chapter. Work in progress.

inquiry which is gendered becoming. She is opening herself to this moving and changing.[15]

For Alex, the allegory is not about the cis/trans binary but is instead reminiscent of Leela Gandhi's notion of "a desire not only for dissolution but for the inauguration of new and better forms of community and relationality hitherto unimaginable."[16]

* * *

If I were younger, my pronouns might well be *they/them*. There are folks my age and AFAB who have made the shift. But I grew up in a world where feminism taught me that my gender—my clothes and presentation, my life decisions, my strength, my desires, and my vulnerability, all of me—could be part of "she," of woman.

The mutual support of the historical butch-femme couple is what I connect/ed with most as a femme. And that mutual support is akin to what I seek and find in my relationship with Alex. While we enjoy some elements of the masc/fem dance, it is being an ally and protector and interlocutor and *listener* that is most important to me. They teach me more about gender, including my own gendering, than I knew was there.

I see "woman" differently now—constructed, not essential, complicated, real and unreal. I see, too, how the feminism that empowered me has often excluded the gendered being—the clothes and presentation, life decisions, strengths and desires and vulnerabilities—of other AFAB people. I am still a feminist, and my "she" pronoun points to both feminist history and my own. The she/her and genderqueer badges side by side on my chest confuse me a bit; can I be both? But both positions feel right for me.

---

15 Alex Nichols, notes for this article.

16 Leela Gandhi, *Affective Communities: Anti-Colonial Thought, Fin-de-Siècle Radicalism, and the Politics of Friendship* (Durham & London: Duke University Press, 2006), 6.

This piece is co-written, inter-written in parts. *Shimmervoyage* is full of passages Alex and I wrote together, both because its story belongs to both of us differently and because there is such pleasure and playfulness in writing together.

Say the limini:
When two become one, there is onelove. It is pleasant enough. But when you become me, and we become you, there is no more 'one,' and time no longer tethers feeling to body. This is the essence of allo, and with it we know the past, share the present and create the future.
You are me
You and me
You are entirely other than me
You share me[17]

17 After Jean-Luc Nancy, as discussed in Leela Gandhi, *Affective Communities: Anti-Colonial Thought, Fin-de-Siècle Radicalism, and the Politics of Friendship* (Durham & London: Duke University Press, 2006), 19.

NOTRE DAME

Llywelyn Lee

when my skull rings empty
like this i want the whole
world to fall on me, to go
up in flames.
like this i dig my fingernails
into the back of my hands,
like this i throb and gasp
from some kind of hunger,
that will not name itself.
i'm thinking about the

walk to your house, your
fingers crawling shyly
into the cavern of my
mouth. if i were someone
different i'd open up wider.
holy molars, consecrated
cerebellum. my heart beats
hard and heavy, weighs
down the centre of my body
like a bell. i'm thinking

about churches.
how even when they're
useless and decrepit, the
bones are still stuffed with
god. we can hear the church
bells from your bedroom. you
roll over and guess the time.
like it doesn't matter if it's

1pm or 9. there is no urgency in this.
just my ear pressed to the
hollow of your belly,
listening to the echo of
you.

PHOTOGRAPHS BY JAN PHILLIPS

NEW LESBIAN WRITING

REFUSING STRAIGHT

Alix L. Olson

Once upon a time, we mistook straight for a kind of people, a boring breed
of breeders, diamond ring and picket fences, you were everything
we'd rejected, all the normal we resented, relentless in convention, you were
in our queer way. We were confronting gendered bathrooms, we were training
to be multiple, if you were straight then you were culpable; straight was your assumptions: "do you have a
boyfriend, honey, what's your boyfriend's name?
the presumptions and the shame: was it something I said to you,
maybe something I read to you; the judgment and forgetting, no plus one
to the wedding.

Straight was the people who asked which one of us wore the pants and then when we laughed- neither if we're
doing it right- they didn't get it, straight was the people who didn't get it. And we didn't really want them to.
We carried comebacks like tazers
tucked inside our cheeks, we policed straight in defense of our lives.

But we mistook straight for people instead of vision, you're not thinking straight, get your head on straight, bracketed vision straight-jackets vision can only see what is straight ahead. It sees justice in a courtroom, possibility in statistics - get your facts straight, let's get one thing straight. Panicked by division, deviation interruption, imprecision, straight vision doesn't dream of other worlds, of other ways.

We mistook straight for people not order, the ordinary order of things, proper order plots the dots, here to there, straight-shot, it doesn't make pit stops to let you pee or ask directions. With the speed of logic and reason it promises away your billion brilliant possibilities: point birth to point death, sacrifice-success, sacrifice-success, no breath, no time for saying wait up, no time for saying hold up when you are all one-way velocity. Straight time is cruel and usual. It's about time, isn't it always about time?

We mistook straight for people instead of sequence, straight sequence disfigures and dis-orders, moves history forward by clear-cutting all that could stumble us, might humble us: read how we've progressed, repeat that we're the best, straight sequence cheerleads and organizes, postures and prosthletizes.

We mistook straight for people instead of business. Straight means business, it stakes its claim in white, makes a wager on white, sustains its share of white, takes hold of whose lives matter, who needs to claim to matter, to cling to the matter, name the color of the matter, straight business is deadly.

We mistook straight for people not production of truth, straight rebukes what coils and twists, insists that Trump will give it to you straight, look you straight in the eye, shoot straight from the hip, straight to the heart of the matter, no qualms, no reservations, no suspicious hesitations, no fancy information or history lessons, no tricky verbs or elitist big words, only clear-cut demands and straight-forward stands, only straight talkers talking straight talk

We mistook straight for a kind of person as if any one being could be any one thing, what a disservice to magic, how tragic to call any being straight: "straight as an arrow," "straight but not narrow," we mistook straight for people not power. Straight is the HRC, brutal equality, power lines that strangle with their intimate parallel force, see straight was never narrow, it widens and accommodates, it despises what it tolerates, in order to stay tidy, it cleans up and legitimates

Straight is the stick figure family on the back of that car, the kids play lacrosse, the moms play guitar, life is good, we're so glad life is so fucking good for you. But refusing straight might mean not settling for the good life, might mean unsettling some forms of good life, might mean refusing to be organized like that, might mean letting down the team, stepping out of party line, disrupting progress, bankrupting the prophets of white.

Refusing straight might mean refusing to un-complicate your vision, might mean your mission statement is a question, might mean insisting that no order is a given, to crooked as a practice, not knowing what will come next, might make you ache for the days when kissing was a protest, was the scene of moral panic, when our slogans made us horny, when our fucking made them frantic, when a rainbow sticker was still a secret wink or a middle finger, when your tribe was comprised of avengers not brides, might make you ache for the days when straight meant them versus us, when our "us" was obvious, when our "us" felt dangerous. When straight meant straight people, confounding straight men, When straight meant straight people, confounding straight girls. Before refusing straight meant taking on the fucking world.

FLIGHT

Jenny Johnson

That summer she and I were chest-deep in a cold river current,
her legs crossed against my lower back, my fingers deep

when seeing a bald eagle soaring above us, tracing the tree line,
I pulled out. Bewildered, she splashed me

with her cupped palm, darted one eyebrow, then teased me
in a way I loved. It must've been jolting,

waves of touch, and then my face swerving
up and out into blue periphery. Hers would swerve, too,

that summer and I'd behave less generously. Both of us
trying something new: perception over possession.

BEAR RUN

Jenny Johnson

How the sun fell as we hiked past the torched buds
of rhododendrons

And now, a boy runs up a boulder
wearing a T-shirt that reads: IGNITE THE BEAST

On our screened-in porch, we read that S/M combines:

"the child's urge for make-believe
with the adult's ability to take responsibility"

I want more privacy, more –

The sun that falls as you kneel on blades of ferns

VISITING WILLA CATHER'S GRAVE, JAFFREY, NH

Liz Ahl

Memorial Day, 2022

In the small portion of shade that dims
this southwest corner of the burial ground,
a lush dappling of bluets blooms a blanket over
Cather's plot and along the slope leading
down to it, as if to light a path. I always
forget bluets aren't forget-me-nots, not
even here, not even when a poem
wishes it so. Like you, perhaps, I was
surprised to learn that she was buried here,
not back in Red Cloud or in New York City.
Like her, I have Nebraska in my past,
and Pittsburgh, too. She wrote a decent swath
of *My Antonia* here in Jaffrey, in a tent
pitched a mile or so from where she and Edith
took rooms most summers. In 1919
the third wave of that famous influenza
caught her as she wrote late summer days
alone at a simple table in that muddy,
dirt-floor tent she loved. No escaping,
we learned, didn't learn, forgot, I forget.
More than two years into the current
pandemic, it still hasn't caught me.
Her marker's so unlikely here, a feeling
of *from away*; most of the other stones
still standing here are thin, grim slate, terse words,
puritanically devoid of sentiment.
Her large, newer headstone: clean, pale granite,

softer at the edges, poetic words as befit
a famous writer and a new century's
notions of death, heaven, sorrow, afterlife.
A fresh rainbow flag's planted in between
the two plain footstones: one for Willa, one
for Edith who died so many years later
but for whom a space had been saved.
I've brought a small red rock from even further
west than Nebraska to set among the others
on the headstone, a crowd of totems
carried here from away, drawn from pockets
and purses, warmed in palms, left as wishes,
as thanks, as prayers, stones tendered to stone.

SHE FINALLY ASKS

Liz Ahl

Twelve hours after you drove me
and the broken bellows of my clotted lungs
to the ER; after you sat and fretted with me
in the tiny room, listening and watching while
they puzzled out the problem; after you helped me
remember and tell the still unfolding story
of my body; after you waited through the comings
and goings for further tests and measurements—

you've finally driven home, left me checked-in
for an open-ended stay, pinned into place
by IV, by whispering cannula and pulse oximeter,
by heart monitor sticky-pads
strategically clinging, listening, listening.

Finally, a nurse asks me the questions
she's mandated to ask, questions
she was trained to wait until you left to ask:
about my safety, my fear, my home.
Some folks read you and me as sisters, not lovers.
Others can't see us, two women together, as real,
and so can't imagine us hurting one another
the way they easily assume straight couples might be
hurting one another, living inside some narrow version
of a marriage's windowless room.

The nurse doesn't have to assume –
she has a form to fill out. She wants to know if I
feel unsafe at home, if anybody there *hurts me*,
and the *no* I give her comes from my very bones,

which don't belong to anybody but myself,
and which know your own bones, even as neither of us
promises the other a future set in stone.

Still, so many years together, I imagine
it was harder for you to have been sent home,
that you might feel more precarious there
than I feel here, in the cradle of all this concern.

I want to ask the nurse what she does
with the *yesses*, broken loose from stoppered throats,
or those she can sense want to emerge
but which get swallowed back down.
Some part of me wants her to inquire next
about who I've hurt, whose safety or happiness
I've valued less than my own. She doesn't ask
about those deep shames, those secrets.

Alone finally, wide awake with all the answers
I gave and all those I didn't have to, I remember
the worry on your face this morning when I said
we need to go to the hospital; you, who have only ever
touched me in ways that awakened me
and reminded me to be alive; you whose care
has woven a net that lets me test my old fears
a little further, lets me leap from a little higher up.

Our home is safer than many other homes,
and yet we know, we've seen with our own eyes,
how peril might find a way in. Not a villain's
shoulder against a bolted door, no specific interloper,
but rather a scratching inside the wall
we've willed ourselves to ignore, or that draft
through the old windows we haven't

replaced yet but meant to. Mean to.
The way a wind we hadn't imagined,
and so couldn't see coming, could press us
together or blow us apart, or both.

LILIA

Frida Clark

the final memories of my abuela are
difficult.
the yellow residue caked around her feeding tube,
the folds of skin almost enveloping themselves—once full of fat
and other body meat— instead reminiscent of deflated balloons.

i think of her often,
other things.
her weakness for solitaire and stray animals, her orange blush,
the way you could see the silver fillings in her molars when she
laughed,

her constant rotation of diets,
diet pills, supplements, teas, exercise machines, tightening
serums, shapewear. once sick, her historic obsession with weight
loss felt particularly painful in retrospect.

we have nearly the same type of body, we gain weight in the
same places. small arms, a flaccid stomach, an almost comically
exaggerated hourglass. sometimes when i look in the mirror or
catch my reflection in a storefront images resurface:
watching her pujar while getting dressed.

it's a death i try to avoid.
but when i build an altar for her on october 31st there's pan dulce,
her almost daily joy with its psychically loaded consumption.

i think now she is free.
we can laugh together,
our chests and bellies heaving at the foolishness
of wasting time on guilt for pleasure.

AN ODE TO JOAN LARKIN

Frida Clark

from the 28th floor of my office building in philadelphia
i see the weather move towards me,
a blurry mass of darkness and humidity.

i think of olivia, on her north carolina coastal plain
facing a similar vision.
instead of height as the illuminating perspective,
she has all-encompassing flatness.

we have been apart for six months.
i have the city
trollies, altercations outside my window after midnight.
she has the country
30 minute drives to the grocery store, snake roadkill that seems
to endlessly regenerate.

at times the thought crosses:
how will we grow old together when we are so far
and she won't even let me chew ice.

but it passes,
quickly,
like the storms we both observe.

DEVOUT

Hadley Grace

I kiss Sophie's head outside our church,
blushing pink as a Sunday School valentine.

Mom says, *Don't kiss your friends.* I burn
baptist-hymnal red. Sophie has a trundle bed,

a swimming pool, eyes bluer
than Noah's flood. She lets me

try on her stick-on earrings.
She's prettier than an Easter dress.

Every girl has a favorite sleepover,
a best best friend. I don't tell her

she is mine.

A gossip of youth group girls swoon
over the future pastor, now in ninth grade.

Sophie says, *He asked for my number!*
The church parking lot cracks

with jealousy. He gets to text her at midnight
while I tear up every diary entry from seventh grade

to seventeen, when the church hallway feels
like winter without snow days. Sophie complains

that she is cold. I hold her hands—
I'll be her softest gloves, the warmest

touch she knows. We play hooky
from youth group, race across the parking lot,

climb into her car and catch our breath.
I'm about to drive away with her

when she drops my hand, uses the warmth
I gave her to wave at her boyfriend.

I want to throw my bible out the window, believe
in her touch instead. But I'm not supposed to dream

about another girl's arms while I sleep
over at her house. I pray myself

awake, stare at her ceiling until
the sun rises on God's wrath.

Maybe I'm dreaming again when Sophie
touches me, asks, *What's keeping you up?*

I leave the amen in my throat,
take my first honest breath and say,

Let's drive. I take us away
from the pastors who said we'd be damned,

past the billboards advertising hellfire.
I don't need their heaven anymore, because Sophie

rolls down the window and laughs loud enough
to drown out the prayers of our parents.

Nobody comes for us.
They're too far gone.

Sophie falls asleep
on my shoulder.

I thank our holy flesh,
kiss her head.

We're too far gone.
We won't go back.

RE-FACING THE KITCHEN CABINETS IN THE HOUSE WHERE I GREW UP

Kristy Bell

A drop of sweat sways at the tip of my nose, and I will it to hold on while I shift the vibrating palm sander in my hand to thumb it to the off position and wipe my face with my t-shirt sleeve. July in south Alabama bears down on my shoulders underneath my Mom's carport. I'm bent over the grease-dappled surface of a kitchen cabinet door, sanding off 50 years of kitchen grime and old paint.

My partner, H, and I decided to re-face the cabinets for Mother's Day this year. We thought we'd start that weekend, then come back in a couple of weeks and finish. The kitchen is small, maybe 10 x 12. No problem.

Instead, Mother's Day weekend marked the beginning of a months-long odyssey of generational torch-passing.

Growing up, I thought everything about our house was embarrassingly half-assed. My Dad's name was Jerry, which lent special double meaning to the term "jerry-rigged." Nothing worked as advertised; nothing was standard. Paint on sections of a wall completed at different times lay down in a mild clash— match-adjacent, instead of a direct match. Daddy generally used what he had, or what he could make himself, in a place where the nearest store of any consequence was 40 minutes away. Even now, the cabinets sport metal hinges he individually whittled to fit within already-installed trim. We've only recently figured out we have to mark them upon removal to get them back on correctly after they're redone.

It strikes me that what we're doing plants us squarely within a long tradition of rural problem-solving. You don't hire some outsider to replace your cabinets in the rural South. You don't replace them at all, if you can help it. If you can't figure out how to *repair* them on your own, you first look for a family member who can do it. If that comes up empty, cast a little wider; maybe somebody from the church can lend a hand. If nobody there knows anything about it, well, aren't we lucky to be living in the YouTube era?

Long before you could learn about such things on the internet, Daddy built these cabinets with his Dad (my PawPaw). Here under the carport, the awareness that every pass of the sander erases brush strokes my ancestors made sits heavy in my gut. A wave of nostalgia rises, and I sing the chorus from Waylon Jennings' "Luckenbach, Texas" aloud. It ebbs. I home in on the circle of grime where the door pull was and see my nine-year-old hand, grubby from clandestine digging in the yard, reaching into the cabinet for a Kool-aid cup.

In the late '60s, PawPaw labored alongside two of his brothers as Jim Walter contractors. A carpenter by trade, he worked for the Tampa-based company off and on, putting up affordable houses throughout the southeast. They'd build out the house shell on already-owned land and leave it for the buyer to figure out the inside, saving money for the new owner, and time for the installers, as the baby boomer generation came of age. When my parents married, my Mom's mother owned 33 acres in rural Barbour County, Alabama, and was only too happy to carve off four acres next door for her daughter, just getting started in life with her new husband.

Mama has never been one to store up her treasures here on earth, so when Daddy died in 2011, she more-or-less resigned herself that whatever Daddy didn't get to before he died would stay broken. When I moved back here from Virginia, to a small town 65 miles away, H and I started breaking down her resignation, one visit at a time. A leaking faucet was the gateway; now, when we come for a bout of cabinet work, she inevitably has a list of minor annoyances she wants handled. She'll wait until I go to the bathroom before mentioning the list to H. My partner tells me and then we confer and plan (and learn how to do whatever it is). In this roundabout way, we've sealed holes, taken off unwanted furnishings, and fixed wiring problems over the past two years.

In most ways, being gay in the deep South is easier than it was 30 years ago, but Mama is bent on saving me from myself and never misses a chance to witness. Some mornings I walk in, and she's poring over the Bible's Sodom and Gomorrah story. This morning when we arrived, she had subtly positioned the weathered Kinney's box that houses my Little Miss Clio tiara and sash in a place where I was sure to see.

"Oh, I just loved when you were in this pageant, didn't you?" she asked.

I grunted and aimed the nail gun into the closet overhead, squeezed the trigger. The gun emitted a satisfying buzz, then whack.

"Do you remember the apricot cream outfit you wore for your interview?"

Another buzz and whack. "Yes, Mother."

"These bows matched the cutest little corduroy jacket." She stroked the bows and reluctantly closed the lid.

H turned toward the wall, so Mama didn't see her laughing. The artifacts are nearly 40 years old, but they may as well be 4,000. I noticed Mama conveniently forgot that they had to pry me out of a tree to put the apricot cream outfit on me.

Under the carport, I think about how Mama believes she's in a battle for my soul and that, if she just prays enough, she can turn me away from my life of sin. I sent her a letter once that explained that it took me years to finally accept who I am, and that I need for her to do that as well. It didn't take. Every few years, we have a falling-out when she goes too far. The most recent one was after I broke up with my last long-term partner. When I told Mama over the phone, she gave a joyful little gasp and said she couldn't be sorry. I hung up and stopped speaking to her for several months. Intellectually, I understand it's her way of loving, but for the disoriented emotional and spiritual parts of me, there's no escaping the orphaned feeling.

In my early 30s, I took to sitting in Daddy's office with him on visits "back home." Mama wouldn't let him drink or smoke in the house proper, so his solution was to build himself an office attached to the house where they could orbit around each other without colliding. One night just before Christmas, he grabbed the keys to his truck and made me drive him around the dirt roads of south Alabama, both of us drinking, him insisting that I tell him what I had to tell him.

I had not planned on telling him anything. I'd been operating under a localized version of the Don't Ask/Don't Tell policy for several years, and I thought it was working just fine. I only saw my parents a couple of times a year, and only for a few days at a time. But he wouldn't let me squirm away from it, so I finally came out to my proud, construction-working, southern man Daddy, several years before Mama figured it out. I thought for sure he would kick me out of the family, but he just hugged me and offered me a cigarette. Later, he would fly to Virginia to stay with my partner and me for several days around my bookstore grand opening.

Mama has largely preserved the office just as Daddy left it, a shrine to the orbit they maintained during his final years. It's come in handy more than once as H and I have had to rummage through drawers to find some tool we forgot to bring. Mama's always had a country person's healthy distrust of the strange, so we've selected a color scheme that's close to what it replaces. We convinced her to let us go a little lighter to make the room look bigger, and we're replacing black hardware with brushed nickel.

I wipe the sanding dust off the cabinet door I'm working on, dip the brush into the open can of paint, and start the back-and-forth plying of the first coat. I can't help but notice the paint is a shade of apricot cream.

NINETEEN EVENING PRIMROSES
Marlee Alcina Miller

A mischievous, crooked, underbite smile.
Last night's blue eyeliner smudged
and fading on her bottom lids.

*

It was the summer I saw 19 evening primroses bloom in real-time.
Stretching their canary yellow petals outward,
as if they're gracing us with a song.

A group of us blew kisses towards them as they shyly opened—
someone told us it helps the process.

*

Her laugh is smoky, and when she plays the accordion
it sounds like Edith Piaf and Janis Joplin had some dreamy love-child.
Auburn curls tumble downwards cascading on top of closed eyelids
as she gets lost in her own song.

When I ask her for a CD, she becomes shy about her voice,
mentioning haggard breathing in between the notes,
as the CD was recorded before she kicked her nicotine addiction.

I don't tell her that I heard her play five years ago and I didn't notice
or maybe, didn't care about any of her insecurities.

What I remember is the heavy footed tapping in rhythm she did
while singing a sea-shanty.

*

I spent most of last night flirting with straight women
who will never kiss me.
I was falling all over myself,
swooning in between gin-flavored hiccups;
when one of her hands lingered on my knee
for an eternity while she laughed.

It made me feel like I want to live forever.

My body is so hesitant and stagnant.
I move with great trepidation through silence.

She is some grand show or a performance.
The kind you don't want people to talk over,
but she doesn't know it.

THE WOMAN AND THE BARDO

Lindsay Rockwell

Nothing and no one else
has survived. Her car is totaled.
She makes out a blur
of bodies— a doe and her fawn,
maybe a man
and a small child form a constellation
splayed on the road. Beyond
the shattered windshield she senses
a vast field, a river
quietly swimming itself through the earth.
The only script she locates
lingers between two worlds.
She wonders about Lazarus.
The bardo. Perhaps he waited too.
She tries to lift a finger—
remembers the precision required to thread a needle.
Notices her breath,
her body, still, as though
hanging. From what she's not sure.
A scene of children dressed in red and yellow flames
running headlong into walls
stuns the corners of her thoughts. But in the center,
a room morphs into focus.
It is cold. Windows open
and blue light floods. The room
becomes a theatre. Her father appears
upstage left. He is made of glass. Softly
spills downstage. Sits
in a glass chair at a glass table
with glass legs. He is smiling, almost laughing.

No time is passing. But backstage
a metronome pulses. Its echo fills the theatre,
saturates the blue light and her glass father.
Everything is porous. How beautiful she thinks—
the incandescent blue, the windows looking
beyond the field swaddling
the swimming river
where snakes, dolphin, stingrays, jellyfish thrive.
Her father reaches for her hand.
The doe and fawn begin
to open their eyes, lift
their heads, shift their stiff, bruised bodies.
Slowly, slowly, they stumble into the field, tall grass swallowing.

RAGE

Lindsay Rockwell

She carries her rage in a glass bottle
rage the color of blood, night—
the shape of heat, wood, steel.

It has a name she cannot say.
It hushes her like rain, like sleep,
so, I carry her rage in a glass bottle.

On horseback, riding scared, we gallop,
our alchemy of dreams sculpts the sky—
dreams the shape of heat, wood, steel.

Heat blows the glass, thunder pounds the steel,
wind whittles wood beneath time's aching arc
and we carry her rage in a glass bottle.

Some nights I watch the blood
work the bottleneck open, remember
her wrist unkindly carved, her

thighs, thorax, scapula— lie
hushed, barely breathing, so yes—
we carry her rage in a glass bottle
rage the color of blood, night.

ULULATION

Lindsay Rockwell

Did you see light wince
when her
body
was ruptured at its root
by a murder
of men

her body   no   her self
became   cleaved   extracted   from her weave
took on   another

she became wind   that did not gather strength   became
mourning
as the disappeared
clouds no longer dressed the sky
unbuttoning their garlands of wet & sheen

she tottered
her mind   a vacant city   her body   a parcel of drought
she searched   beneath petals   sipped
from cactus   drank   tea of the ayahuasca
became   the shape of nothing   sound of sand

then   wind gently gathered strength
inside her
she wrung her hands   slowly   slowly   wrung her hands
their maps   of deserts   & cracked earth   rubbing
until her skin   no   sinew   no   her fascia

yes
began to unwind

yes
reverse direction
her tortured self
became a mountain
a field
where lupin and acacia
ululate to clouds to come out
of their corners
rain the sweet sweat of rain

I, MOUNTAIN

Lindsay Rockwell

I woke this morning a mountain.
What I mean is I woke and found
my body to be a mountain. This was unexpected
and spectacular. A mountain
breathing with a four chambered heart
holding raven's sky. I mean
ravens are holding up the sky
and the sky is in my mountain heart
and though my heart has only four chambers
each is infinite and curious. The first chamber
holds all my mother's kites.
Holds my mother's kites
close to my mountain skin, wind
and ocean salt. And as the unbreakable dawn
declares herself, I, mountain, am now weeping
because I am also a body that is human
and very small, with a four chambered
heart that impossibly pumps, holds the strings and sees
the streamers of all my mother's kites
boundless as sky and salt and let's not forget the stars.

THE QUIET WAR

Lindsay Rockwell

When you feel words
& silence
stripped from your throat

when you bare your breasts
& smell
the no return

when your fragments, dark & loaded
shatter, as
prism light & when

you finally find the quiet war
inside you
it is then, your unknown

sisters and your brothers call
& call
yes you you you

we see you, filled
with fear
& rain, frozen

at your final border, the grim & poem
of you
leaning, calling too

OGYGIA

Serrana Laure

Streetlamps poured liquid gold across the wet cobblestones, staining the city ochre. A pregnant moon slung low over the cathedral on the hill, minting the rain clouds in silver.

"Does everything here look like a movie set?" Aster said.

Matteo smiled and put his hand on her knee. A tickle of pleasure skittered across her skin, happy to be reunited with the warmth of his touch after two long months of separation. This was his first trip home since their green card interview; his first trip home in over ten years. The day his papers arrived in the mail, he'd booked his ticket for three-months. Aster had only been able to take off three weeks but was excited to be here anyway. They'd fought just before he left but she wasn't really sure why and they hadn't talked about it since. He murmured something about the town's obligation to keep things historic. The rain increased its tempo on the roof of the car. Matteo slowed, skidding on the wet stones. Aster's head lolled, bouncing against the window with a thud. They'd been driving over an hour already and bed called to her like siren song.

Matteo had been telling her about his hometown since the day they met. "To understand all that is me," he said, "You must see Sicily." He loved to tell her stories from the *old country*, though he always said this with a bit of a smirk. He'd left his motherland twelve years ago, and yet, he spoke of it as if *home* were synonymous with *personhood*. Aster found this notion strange. Having left Ohio when she was just eighteen, she'd never really thought about what being from there meant, how it was a part of her cultural identity. Rather, she had tried to transform *Midwesterner,* into *New Yorker,* as fast as she possibly could. Though there was more glamour to saying, *I'm from Sicily,* than saying, *I'm from Ohio.* Now, looking out at the rain-soaked streets, she thought she understood, just a little bit, his nostalgia for home—the crooked stone buildings, the turmeric light, the tang of Mediterranean salt crystalizing on her lips.

She ran her fingers through the patch of duckling fuzz on the right side of her head, it would be unruly in no time. She should have buzzed it before she left. After five years of marriage, she'd finally made it here to meet his people, she couldn't look like a disheveled mess.

When they arrived at his childhood home, his parents were thankfully already sleeping. She'd met them once before when they came to visit Matteo in New York and liked them. They were all hugs and kisses and demands that she eat—*mangia, mangia*. Their kindness and love for her transcended the fact that she, nor they, understood a fucking word the other said. Or rather, they loved her, she suspected, largely because they *didn't* understand her. She collapsed into bed and Matteo laid down beside her.

He buried his face in her hair and whispered, "I missed the way you smell."

The following morning, she woke to a waft of coffee from the other room. She reached for Matteo, but he was no longer in bed. She laid there alone, in the fuzzy polyester sheets, listening to the melody of language she could not understand creeping under the door.

—

Friday evening the entire family gathered at one long table, thirty of them: aunts, uncles, cousins, nieces, nephews, second cousins. She couldn't keep track of names, so she just smiled. First came the gnocchi, made from scratch; then the lasagna, also homemade; then the horse meat—a Sicilian delicacy conjured just for her.

Matteo examined her as she took her first bite of horse. "You like? They want to know," he said.

"Si, bene," she said.

"Buono," he corrected. "Bene means everything is good. Buono means it tastes good."

"Buono," she said, forcing a smile. The cousins laughed at her accent but clapped her on the back and congratulated her mother-in-law for winning over the American. Why did she feel so uncomfortable? Was it simply that she couldn't understand what they were saying about her? Was it the way the cousins touched her tattoos without asking, and rubbed the fuzzy side of her head, and muttered to one another, as though they'd never seen anything like her before? Was it the way her mother-in-law stared at her across the table—not like she was judging her, exactly, but like she was trying to solve a puzzle? What puzzle? Was she trying to figure out what her son saw in a heavily tattooed, half-bald, blue-haired woman? Was it none of it and all of it at once?

"You like Sicilia?" One of the cousins asked in his best English.

"Si. Molto," she responded. "Very much. Bello." She blushed. Despite her best efforts to learn it, Italian felt wrong in her mouth, too round, like she was holding a golf ball in the back of her throat. Her perfect French helped with comprehension but did her no favors with pronunciation.

The pitter patter of words and laughter swirled and swaddled her. She'd never known her cousins; both her parents had left their homes behind and never gone back. She closed her eyes.

She was jerked out of the non-place in which she was floating— somewhere between the beach and her lasagna—by someone handing her a moist squirming, infant. What was she supposed to do with an infant? She held him six inches from her body as though she might break him and tried to bounce him up and down and smile, while everyone at the table babbled at her. About her?

"They ask you if you want kids," Matteo said.

"Tell them I most certainly do not," she said. He gave her a look that said, *but I thought you said maybe*, and she grimaced. Anger welled, ferric at the back of her throat. How dare he put her in a situation like this?

"Quando vivrai qui?" Cousin number seven—the one who had handed her the baby—was asking her something. She looked at Matteo to translate.

"She wants to know when will we move here," he said, but he was speaking quieter now, sensing the anger rippling off her like heat. She wasn't sure exactly why she was so angry, except that she had a general aversion to being cornered and was trying her absolute best to be polite. She wanted to scream, *I'm never moving here, and I don't want kids, and your son should have told me he did before he married my ass in the first place.* They were all still staring at her. Did they know what she was thinking? Hadn't she smiled? Wasn't she always smiling? The baby in her arms was screeching, she realized. The youngest of the cousins, with her wild curls and wire framed glasses got up from her seat and came over.

She took the baby from Aster's arms saying, "Lascia in pace, la povera donna." She handed the baby back to his mother and turned back to Aster. "Sorry. They no have, how you say, maniere. I Chiara. Later we drink." She winked and Aster flushed. Chiara was pretty, unfairly so, and of everyone here, she looked the most like Matteo—more like a sister than a cousin. Aster tried to give some indication of her gratitude, but static churned through her brain. She took a gulp of wine.

Finally, after many more rounds of food, dinner was over. Aster didn't say anything on the ride home. She could feel Matteo sneaking glances at her in his periphery, but he did not speak. As they pulled into the driveway, she said, "I'm going for a walk on the beach."

The summer light lingered, even at this hour, casting a lavender glow on the flat oil slick of the sea. She sat on a crooked stone wall soothed by the sound of waves lapping the edge of the pier. Why had the interaction with the baby rattled her so? Was it really about not wanting kids or was she just frustrated that she couldn't speak for herself? Or was it something else entirely? The sound of footsteps pulled her out of the whirlpool of her thoughts. Matteo handed her a beer and sat down next to her.

"I'm sorry," he said. "I didn't mean to put you on the spot. My family..." he trailed off.

"I just really don't appreciate being cornered. And what was all that talk about us moving here? Do you want to move back here?"

"No. I, I think, sometimes. I miss my people. Ma, no. I don't. I love our life." He kissed the top of her head. She should have felt comforted by his proclamation that he was happier with her, in their life, but something that felt suspiciously like dread curdled in her stomach.

—

Aster waited in the car for Matteo to come out of the grocery store. They were babysitting his three-year-old nephew and she'd agreed to wait with him while Matteo shopped for dinner. She scrolled through Instagram and regretted it immediately. These days, her entire feed consisted of nothing more than people virtue signaling about their politics and showing off their ten-thousand-dollar engagement rings. The same people who talked to so much about wanting to make the world a better place, and wealth re-distribution, and socialism, and blah blah blah, flaunted their privilege without batting their eyelash extensions. How had she ever been friends with these people? Then she felt a tapping, a poking rather, in the meat of her upper arm.

"Zia. Zia," Alessandro said, *Aunty.* He was calling her aunt. Her stomach squiggled. "Cos'è questo?" He was pointing to something on the back seat. She stuck her head through the middle to see what he was referring to. A roll of paper towels, not something she knew how to say in Italian.

She shook her head. "Non lo so. I don't know. I'm sorry." He looked up at her, disappointed, like, because she was an adult, she was supposed to know everything, and why didn't she even know how to speak to him? Was she stupid? Her skin grew hot. She opened her mouth to speak again, but the words stuck at the back of her throat. Just as he started to make a face like he was going to cry, the door opened. Matteo was back, thank god. He cooed at his nephew, calming him with tenderness in his deep voice.

—

At the ruins of Agrigento, the copper-green man lay on his side, giant and limbless, in front of the nearly intact Temple of Concordia—the sky so blue it hurt to look.

"These are some of the best-preserved Greek, how you say, rovine?"

"Ruins?"

"Yeah, *ruins* which exists," Matteo said. "You know, Ulisse."

"Yeah, I love the Odyssey. I can't believe I'm looking at this shit in real life. Like, can you even call something a ruin if it's basically fully intact?"

Matteo smiled at her. "Come, let's see the garden." They wandered through the labyrinth of terraced gardens, holding hands. She pointed out plants she knew, and asked questions he did not have the answers to about the ones she'd never seen before. She didn't mind that plants weren't his thing; he indulged her. At the top of the hill, she stopped suddenly, panting, the heat of the sun scratched at the back of her neck where a sunburn was starting. They sat on a low stone wall gazing out over the Mediterranean which stretched turquoise from the bottom of the sloping hills out past the horizon.

"That way is Tunisia?" she asked, pointing.

"Yep. At night, you sometime can see the lights," Matteo said.

"Wow." As she stood there, staring at the invisible coast of Tunisia, she found herself overtaken with the immensity of history, and a feeling that she was at once entirely insignificant and inextricably connected to it all. These ruins had been there for thousands of years, built to worship the gods of old, so powerful they themselves had become imbued with the magic of myth. How many millions of people had come to this place throughout the centuries? What rituals had been performed here? What spells had been cast? She put her hand on a stone, heat creeping into her.

"Do you ever think about how we're connected to the people that built these?" she asked. Matteo shrugged. She sighed. He had plenty of interesting qualities; waxing poetic about the connectedness of humanity was not one of them. She thought back to the day of their green card interview when the interviewer asked her what they had in common, and she'd answered instead that she thought their marriage was made strong by their differences rather than their similarities; that they taught each other things. She hadn't thought much about it since, but now she found herself wondering why she couldn't answer such a simple question. Did they really not have anything in common? Hadn't they once? Or had they just been in a moment in their lives in which sharing fancy dinners and staying up till dawn drinking expensive wine and chain smoking, had felt like enough? She leaned over and kissed him, tongue lingering, letting him pull her close with a hand in the small of her back, the other tangled in her hair. They hadn't talked about their fight on the eve of his departure, and part of her wanted to bring it up, to understand why he'd been so angry at her, but the answers she was looking for might not be the ones she wanted.

—

The barbershop could have been any barber shop, except that every seat was full of strapping, olive skinned men who looked at her as though she was the most beautiful and strange creature they'd ever seen. Matteo and his cousins bantered in dialect as they steered her into a chair and wrapped her in a poncho. He gestured with his hands, indicating the side of her head she wanted to shave.

"How short you want?" he asked her.

"Like, almost all the way bald?" she said. Her undercut had become untenable. Matteo nodded and babbled something to the kid with the buzzer. Her Italian was getting better, but her Sicilian was shit. A murmuring spread down the line of men. "Oh, come on," she said, "I can't be the only person in Italy with an undercut." In the mirror, she caught a glimpse of curly hair and glasses lurking in the shadows of the hallway.

"Chiara!" Lorenzo, the Francophile cousin who was cutting her hair said, "ça c'est ma cousine, aussi."

"Oui, je sais. Je l'ai rencontrée la semaine dernière," Aster responded. *I met her last week.* She found it both funny and a little bit exciting that here, in this country she had never been to before, the only language anyone had in common with her was her father tongue. It made her miss her dad, though he had been dead for years now, but it also made her feel—in the same way she imagined Matteo might feel when he spoke of home— connected to the place of her ancestors. "Ciao Chiara," she said, and waved.

Chiara stepped out of the shadows and said, "Cosa stai facen-do?" Though she smiled at Aster in a way that said, *I know exactly what you're doing, and good for you for holding your own with all these boys.* The men erupted in a cacophony of explanation, gesturing to the side of her head, laughing, and patting her on the back. She couldn't quite tell if they were making fun of her or en-amored with her. Her tattoos continued to be quite the topic of conversation as well. It was as though they'd never seen anyone quite so tattooed before, but that wasn't true; plenty of the men surrounding her had more than one themselves. She felt like she had somehow stepped back in time. She raised an eyebrow at Matteo.

He kissed the top of her head and said, "They love you, don't worry." His "ohs" always sounded like, "uhs" in words like *worry*, which she loved. The way he spoke was one of the things she'd first loved about him. He had his own turns of phrase, neither English nor Italian. He loved to say, *I can't stand close to her,* when what he meant was, *I can't stand her.* This one was her favorite because it seemed, to her, to be even more accurate—*I dislike her so much that I literally do not want to be near her.* She'd felt this feeling intensely and often. She never corrected him when he said things like this; they were part of who he was, and his English was good enough, really.

Later that night as they lay in the unpleasantly furry sheets of the guest bedroom, Matteo rolled on top of her and started kissing her in the way he always did when he wanted to have sex. Despite her discomfort at having his parents right on the other side of the wall, she missed the way he made love to her—the way he breathed into her neck and whispered her name, the smell of his skin. But this time when he pulled her close and she closed her eyes, she saw a nymphlike smile framed by a mess of curls, eyes full of mischief. As she came, the vision solidified into a face, a face she should not be thinking about while having sex with her husband. Afterwards, as Matteo buried his face in her hair, she rolled onto her side, trying to suppress the panic rising hot and sticky in the back of her throat.

—

"Who puts fries on pizza?" Aster said.

"It's tradition," Matteo said, then turned to cousin Alessio to translate. Alessio mumbled something in Sicilian and Matteo laughed. "He says it's not just tradition, it's delicious, so why care?"

Aster raised an eyebrow. "I mean, sure, who doesn't want carbs with their carbs? I get it." Her stomach twisted as though in response to her question. It had been at least two weeks since she'd eaten a vegetable.

"So, after this, we will go drink with Alessio?" Matteo said, but it was not a question. She didn't want to be a buzz kill but between her stomachache and not understanding anything they were saying all evening, she wasn't really feeling up to it. Plus, it was already past midnight.

"Why don't you guys go out and I'll meet you at home?"

"You know how to drive a, how you say it, manual?"

"Yes darling, I'm aware that you only know me in the city, but I do, in fact, know how to drive." She'd meant for this to sound playful, funny even, but the words tasted bitter on her tongue and Matteo didn't laugh.

"Okay. Whatever makes you happy." But he didn't sound happy when he said this and Aster was again, struck by the feeling that something had gone sideways between them, though she couldn't explain why. They'd been together for almost six years now, but she still felt like there was a part of him she would never understand. She'd hoped this trip would make their marriage stronger, that seeing where he came from would help her crack the code of who he really was underneath his pretty face, and endearing accent, and good taste in wine. But instead, she felt something slipping, as though he was reverting to the person, he had *been* instead of the person she knew. They'd had a whole ordeal earlier that day when Aster tried to do her own laundry—his mother had gotten upset. This scared her. She didn't want to be married to someone who needed his mother to do his laundry and expected her to do the same. Even thinking this made her feel mean, like she was judging him, which she wasn't, at least not intentionally. Rather, she got mean when she felt trapped and being here, in this place, this family—where everyone had kids or wanted them; where the women just did the housekeeping no questions asked and seemed happy about it; where the boys lived with their mothers until they lived with their wives—made her feel like a caged beast. If Matteo thought bringing her here would make her change her mind about having a family, he'd been mistaken. But why was she even thinking this way? He'd never tried to manipulate her before, why would he now? Why not just talk to her? Or maybe she was just projecting all of it because she was insecure and being around his family made her feel scrutinized. *Stop being a child, Aster,* she said to herself. *Talk to your husband.*

Matteo and Alessio stood in the street and watched her try to squeeze out of the tiny parking spot. She really didn't want to jerk into the Lamborghini parked in front of her. The men gestured with their hands, trying to help her, even though Matteo knew this kind of "help" made her irrationally angry. Again, she couldn't help but feel judged, like her desire to do things like drive herself home and wash her own fucking laundry made her somehow uncouth. She finally got out of the parking spot and waved out the window at the two men. Driving home, she was struck, yet again by the unreality of the place. The medieval stone buildings and the honey light. The way you could smell the sea even when you couldn't see it.

She pulled into the driveway and got out of the car. She slid the key into the lock and turned; the door did not open. She tried another key; the door still did not open. She put the first key back in the lock and turned the other direction; the lock did not budge. *Shit,* she thought. *Shit. Shit.* She tried the first key again, to no avail. She pulled out her phone and called Matteo. It went straight to voicemail. What the fuck was she supposed to do now? She couldn't ring the doorbell and wake up her in-laws; it was one in the morning. She sat on the steps and gazed at the stars. Raindrops pricked her face. *Fantastic.* She huddled against the archway of the building trying to stay dry. Just as she was about to ring the doorbell and wake up Matteo's parents, Chiara turned the corner. Her massive mess of curls caught the amber light through the mist, giving her a halo. She smiled when she saw Aster.

"Ciao," she said.

"Ciao," said Aster. She hoped the rain would conceal the fact that she was blushing.

"You, no have—" Chiara gestured with her right hand, attempting some kind of universal signal for key.

"Key?" Aster held up the keys and shrugged. Chiara raised an eyebrow and put out her hand. Aster handed her the keys, but she was already shaking her head.

"No the key," she said, gesturing to the door, then jerking her head at Matteo's Aunt's house across the street. "Vieni con me," she said, taking Aster's wrist. Heat roiled through Aster, making her head spin as though she'd been drinking. She put a hand on the stone wall of the building, trying to steady herself. Chiara tugged her through a side door and into the tiny kitchen of her parents' house.

Light from the streetlamp outside slipped through the diaphanous curtains gilding Chiara's cheekbones, the droplets of rain glinting like metal in the half light. She smiled and every inch of Aster's skin went hot again, then cold. She shivered and Chiara cocked her head and bit her bottom lip. She opened a cabinet to the left of the stove and pulled out a bottle of Amaro. She held it out to Aster, asking, without words if she would like some.

Say no, a voice deep inside her whispered, but even as she began to shake her head, her lips formed the words, "Si. Grazie."

The first sip hit her in a wave of sweet, then bitter, and she licked her lips, savoring the sticky richness of herbs she could not name. They stood there, dripping on the marble, saying nothing and drinking, for a moment that stretched between them, strong yet fragile like sinew pulled tight, neither of them knowing what to say to each other in their cobbled together language of broken phrases.

Aster finished her drink and Chiara reached out to refill her cup, but this time when she touched her hand, her fingers grasped instead of grazed, and she stepped closer. She laced her fingers with Aster's, holding the cup between them, her eyes coruscating with what, exactly? Doubt? Hunger? Desire? She took another step closer. They were only two inches apart now and Aster could feel the warmth of Chiara's breath on the chilly skin of her cheeks. Then, there was no space between them, and as their lips met, something in Aster she had not known she'd been ignoring inflated, then bloomed and began to burn; a long dormant desire, frightening, and yet, though her conscious mind was quiet, something akin to relief unfurled deep within her, as though she had finally cracked some kind of unbreakable code—an answer to a question she had never thought to ask.

Chiara's hands were roaming now, expertly working buttons and zippers. She put her lips into the nape of Aster's neck, taking the skin between her teeth, gently, yet strong enough to make her gasp. Chiara put her hand over Aster's mouth and murmured, "Tranquillamente. I miei genitori."

Chiara's hands found their way to the waistband of her jeans, and she paused for a moment, her eyes asking the question her lips could not, and Aster nodded and begged, "Si. Per Favore. Si."

Chiara bent her over the kitchen counter and Aster clutched at the edge and pressed her face to the cool marble as all the things she thought she knew about pleasure inverted and her knees went limp. Then they were on the floor, and she was gasping, begging for more, more, please more, and Chiara obliged, and just as Aster thought she could not take it anymore, the last thread of her control slipped from her and her whole body flooded with something so intense that later, when she tried to tell her best friend about it, she could only describe it as feeling like she had touched magic, and her vision burst into a galaxy of tiny twinkling lights and she sighed into Chiara's neck. They laid there entwined on the floor panting for a long time.

The sound of a cell phone vibrating against the counter jerked Aster back to reality. She jumped up, panic rising acidic in her throat, and grabbed her cellphone. The screen was alight with Matteo's smile. Still naked, she answered the phone, trying to sound normal, but she felt like a snared rabbit; her eyes darted around the kitchen groping for an escape, but the thing she was trying to escape was not this room—it was not even this house or this country, or this situation—and this realization flooded her with an anguish so intense it took everything she had to not start sobbing right there.

"Where are you?" He sounded worried.

"I'm across the street. The key didn't—it was raining—your cousin—" she was babbling. "I'm coming right now," she finished, as she scrambled into her jeans. The last thing she wanted was for Matteo to come here looking for her.

"Okay," he said. "I'll wait for you downstairs."

Chiara watched as she tugged her boots on and stumbled to the door. As she put her hand on the doorknob, Aster turned to look one last time at Chiara's face; she was smiling a half smile, but the light that had reached out from behind her eyes to embrace Aster mere moments before, had gone out. She reached up and touched Aster's cheek with two fingers and whispered, "Ciao." And Aster knew this was not the *see you later,* kind of ciao but rather, the *see you never again,* kind. Something in her gut twisted and she gasped and quickly turned away.

Aster stepped onto the street and turned her face up into the rain, praying for, what exactly? Salvation? Something had been unlocked in her tonight and she was teeming with the kind of emotion she had not felt in years. Exhilaration and guilt thrummed through her, and she knew she had just stepped over the kind of line she could never step back across, into some feral awakening. She pulled her jacket tighter around her and hustled across the street to where Matteo was standing in the doorway of his parents' house.

"You're soaked," he said.

"Yeah, I sat on the steps for a while before Chiara found me."

"Why didn't you call me?"

"I did. It kept going to voicemail."

"I'm sorry, my love," he said and hurried her inside.

"I'm freezing," she said, "I'm gonna shower." She marveled at her brain's capacity to come up with a lie before she even realized she was lying. Where had she learned that? Matteo nodded and leaned in to kiss her.

"Goodnight," he said and smiled. He turned to go, then turned back to her. "You smell different," he said.

Aster shrugged. "Different country, different smell," she said, though she could not quite meet his eyes. He gazed at her for another moment, then turned and walked into the bedroom.

She stepped into the heat of the shower, shaking. Her body twinged with soreness, and she didn't know whether to cry or laugh ecstatically. What had just happened? Had she entered a wormhole and come out the other side as someone else?

Matteo was already sleeping when she came to bed. She climbed in beside him, fully clothed and stared into the dark. Memories of the evening flashed across her vision, as though projected on the ceiling above her: Chiara's lips parting just before she leaned in to kiss her, hands in her hair pulling her head back just so, the heat of their bodies against the cold of the marble floor. She pressed her eyelids shut, begging for sleep to save her from the sickly feeling of guilt curdling in her. But even her dreams were feverish and exhilarating.

—

Their last few days with his family passed in a blur, packed with meal, after meal, after meal with family members Aster still could not name. She was grateful for once, for her inability to speak; finding solace in her silence, she let herself slip into the non-place. Matteo was in his element, always charming, always the golden child, the one with the exciting American life, and she smiled and drank wine, she was good at that at least. Chiara was nowhere.

On the plane ride home, she said very little. She didn't know what she was supposed to say. Matteo chatted inconsequentially to the person sitting next to them, then drifted off with his head on her shoulder. She gazed at him, face calm, framed in dark curls, and swallowed the salt gathering at the back of her throat. All she could think was, *we were happy. We were happy, once.*

ONE HUNDRED LESBIANS

Deborah Seddon

After Wisława Szymborska

When was I last with one hundred lesbians?
One hundred women who love women?

Jozi Pride, 2011.
High as a balloon on E and leaping
for the sky at Zoo Lake.

Lira womans onto the stage
and sings us "Pata Pata."
Everyone whoops and stamps.
We leap on the flat dry grass.

One hundred lesbians? More.

Queer women everywhere.
It's as queer as the eye can see.

The shirtless firemen on their float.
The BDSM peeps with their studs and whips.

The thin old white guy who
joins our table in the sun
doesn't say a word.

When we say hello
he holds up a cardboard sign
that reads "Born this Way"
and smiles without his teeth.

Me in my new blue jeans
and the dark brown t-shirt
that was a gift from a friend:

Dip me in chocolate and
throw me to the lesbians.

Brand new. Freshly hatched.
38 and never been kissed
— by a girl.

(No. There was that one time,
that truth-or-dare game, that undergrad party.
It made me so afraid of myself).
But here I am at last in my
new blue jeans and my new
chocolate shirt standing in
the queue for the portaloo in
my shweshwe hat.

And a beautiful girl with wide
dark eyes asks me if this is the queue.

When I reply she smiles and says
"Oh you're so cute! Can I give you a kiss?"

When I say yes, she kisses each of my cheeks.
Then another girl says, "Oh me too please."

Suddenly here they are.
Women putting their arms around me.
Oh all the lovely beaming and kissing!

Alone in the portaloo, I can
hardly stand. I look at myself

in the tiny square of mirror
hooked over the basin
on the blue plastic wall.

My face is covered in lipstick.
Kisses in pink, in red, in brown
and purple and green. The pupils
of my eyes are enormous.

I took a selfie of the new
me in a portaloo
at ten past three.
My pupils wide with Ecstasy.

38 and just covered in kiss.
Tell me, who could have pictured this?

So let's take one hundred lesbians.

Those who knew from very young they were, somehow different?
Seventy-eight.

Those who knew exactly who they were as children
and became gold star lesbians?
Fifteen, maybe. (Statistics here will depend on the letter of their
generation.)
Those who were tomboys and different from the other girls
but went on to marry a man and have children?
Fifty-eight (maybe more).

Those who never considered themselves queer but one day, to
their surprise,
found themselves in love with a friend?
Thirty-two.

Those who came out to their families, to be accepted and loved
without questions asked?
Two.

Those who were bullied by parents, peers, and teachers?
Ninety-eight.

Those who have been raped, harassed, or assaulted because they
are lesbians?
Fifty-six.

Those who have been raped, harassed, or assaulted because they
are women?
Eighty-four.

Those who have been with more than one man and wonder if they
are permitted
to embrace the name of "lesbian"?
Seventy-seven.

Those who embrace "queer" as a better term for themselves?
Sixty-three.

Those who sometimes wish they weren't queer?
Thirty-five

Those who feel being queer is the best thing in the world?
Forty-two.

Those who beat themselves up for leaving it all so goddamn late?
Eighty-nine.

Those who decide to transition to somewhere non-binary or fluid?
Twenty-one.

Those who live with self-hatred that surfaces without warning?
Ninety-eight.

Those for whom it sometimes surfaces, what they really want,
but who've decided it is either too late or too difficult to come out?
Thirty-four.

You cannot take one hundred lesbians and tell their stories in
numbers.
All models are subjective.
Besides, I'm a poet, not a mathematician.

At one point, we all might have been any of these women.

Except (of course)
those lucky two.

COLOR DANGER

Susan Spilecki

"God made gender an infinite playground." --Stacey Waite
"Letter from Thomas Beattie to the Media"

I know butches who refuse to wear any shade of pink,
detest floral fabric, eschew earrings, insist on boxer
briefs. It can be dangerous to appear soft, disempowering
to show up as the "gentler" gender. We remember
all too well, junior high when we began to be schooled
in dresses, makeup, legs and feet cold four seasons,
and for what? Boys didn't have to make sacrifices.

In the 1980s, I'd never heard of drag, but if I had,
O if I had, what explosion of comprehension might--
But I didn't. The not-my-body/not-my-face went on.
After the dance, I'd peel it off, shake myself like a dog
pull on my human clothes like my real skin again. So
I understand my butch friends' sartorial consternation,
clothing qualms, the distress of the distaff dressing room.

Their trial on the men's side of the department
store is physical; they judge their feet too small,
their legs and arms too short, their shoulders too
slender. And when they do find a shirt, say, or shorts
to try on and they see the lip-sticked dragon in between
the pink side and the blue, there is an anxious moment
when they have to choose. Either way, she'll frown.

Growing up, we played on monkey bars with
abandon, chittering monkeys climbing, swinging.

If you fell, there was always plaster and multicolored
names inscribed. These days, parents aren't so
sanguine about their children's blood. Back then,
women I never met got shoved in bars and skating
rinks. Women wearing pants were assumed dykes

until proven otherwise. A man's fear is gunpowder.
His muscles are leaden slugs. Now everyone and
their grandmother wears jeans, indigo a neutral
color. Danger is a cultural construct, like identity,
shifting shoals, now uncovered here, submerged
there. The Earth spins in slow motion; the world
follows slowly behind. A friend once gave me seeds:

morning glory, cleome, clematis: purple, pink,
lavender, magenta. Coming out, I planted them
in my closet. Watered, they climbed up the walls,
took their rightful place up and down my neckties,
bowties, silken pocket squares. Now the straight
women in the restroom blink, smile, compliment me
on my style. What can I say? Ladies like flowers.

WHAT BECKONS, WE CANNOT ALWAYS SAY

Carla Schick

after Tudor Arghezi's *Song*

I argue with logic but no hope
and slide far away
over a full moon's shadow,
unbelievable lunacy.
I build dams from dirt and forge
gulfs within us.

In the sky we still hold hands

Distant howls   shivering swirls of cloud
banks. I visit, pace pathways—
Unspeaking comrade   Touch
marbled stones safe in my hand.

At the creek, you soak a cloth
taken from your grandmother's house,
a needlework of lace and daisies,
wipe my brow and rest
my face in your cool hands.

You wander into the water and reveal
your body, beckon me
to follow and wade
in freezing waters.

You seek winter's remains
of ice and lean to drink
when your mouth catches mine.

We wander into a turning
Spring flowers bud—

If we spoke, the same words would fall
from our lips—

I squint into our reflections in the tumult
of a new waterfall—

Birds sing
what I cannot.

LETTER WRITTEN WAITING FOR A PLANE IN THE MEXICO CITY AIRPORT

Carla Schick

Impossible that I lost
my travel visa. I went through my wallet,
searched my body for that thin paper
folded into quarters, my signature neat
and squared off. I emptied my pockets
inside out while pilots & flight attendants
rolled by trailing their suitcases
grating tracks of noise on hard floors.

I cannot leave
without identification,
must turn in what has been misplaced—

> On the Paseo de la Reforma,
> just a day before, I hailed a cab for you
> told the cabbie
> *Ella quiere ir al aeropuerto,*
> from the International terminal,
> and left out
> what you'd never say—
> your desire to depart,
> wordless hands waving
> goodbye. You turned back
> for a second. I saw your face
> in the rear window,
> sad eyes following me
> to nowhere.

Now, days after, when I stand ready
to turn in my ticket, the woman, working these lines

of people, tries to listen
to my anguish. I am invisible
without proof of my visit, my name
dissolves in a baby's cries
behind me and a mother grasps the edge
of her stroller, bends down to tell her child, in loud
tones, *shhh.* The mother turns
looking, right to left, covering her shame
with palms that cup her baby's chin,
while the woman from Mexicana reminds me
hay un problema in my going, trapped in my own
absurdity, no place to return to, not even home
as she leads me down an endless hallway,
like a gangplank falling

into the mouth of a shark, to a tiny room
where, I imagine, some man will ask me
how can you be so stupid? his lips moving,
flickering fluorescent lights, buzzing
a raspy radio with signals interrupted
and straining to reach me. I hear
only silence, no sounds
travel across us. He checks the photo
on my passport, decides it is a likeness
and hands me permission to depart, a visa
stamped duplicate. I am a copy

of myself, sipping an espresso
in the café, making it last for hours as I peer into
arrivals & departures, worldwide
passengers. Who gets to stay,
who is left behind? I write in my journal
poems I will not remember writing, and a letter
never sent, rising up with the momentum

of a plane gaining speed to escape
a whirl of mountain winds.
I look back at dust
and imagine our bodies
joined as the twin volcanoes,
holding hands against what wears
us down over time.

GERALDINE FROM PHILLY

Kathy Anderson

Geraldine was a little buzzed from her afternoon martini, actually a big glass of pure gin with fat green olives bobbing in it. She kept herself well-lubricated, starting her day with a glass of prosecco, having white wine with lunch, a cocktail mid-afternoon, red wine with dinner, and a brandy before bed. The best antidote to the crap that came with aging was a steady stream of alcohol, she found.

Once she turned seventy-five, Geraldine found that knowing she could die at any moment made life very dramatic. It was like an excited dog ran by her side all the time. Was this the day she keeled over on a bus, felled by an aneurysm careening around her brain? Would her heart stop while she sat on a bench in Rittenhouse Square enjoying a double gelato? Or would she have a fatal stroke right on the sidewalk in front of her rowhouse like her neighbor Sumi had?

She was on her way to her favorite Italian deli when she felt a very strange feeling, like the hands of the universe were pulling the air tight around her. What was about to happen? She looked around, confused. *I don't hear sirens, no one is running, there's no reason for me to feel on high alert but I am.*

Then a man leaned over and vomited a copious amount of orange liquid all over the sidewalk and kept on walking as though nothing had happened. The orange puddle spread and spread wider, making everyone step into the street to avoid it, like shore birds scurrying from an incoming wave. At the same time, a swarm of pre-teen boys on bikes rode down the middle of Broad Street stopping traffic, throwing their bodies into backbends with the bike still moving, using their hands on the pavement as brakes, doing high wheelies, and then disappearing around a corner like geese in V-formation flying away. Next, a grinning man with tattoos covering his neck shouted, "I'll hold you down and piss on you," at his little boy who yelled back, "Then I'll POOP all over you." Finally, a big dog with a whole ear of corn sticking out of its mouth trotted down the street all by itself, looking for all the world like a fat man chewing on an unlit cigar.

This was exactly why she loved living in the city, it was so *interesting.* But she had never seen this many crazy things all happening at the same time before. This was not right. Overcome by all the commotion, Geraldine briefly forgot where she was going; she edged to the nearest building and put her back against a wall. She refused to be one of those old people who blocked sidewalks, oblivious to their impact on others.

It all felt so mystical and meaningful to Geraldine—the orange vomit, the upside-down boys on bikes, Tattoo Dad and his son, the dog with the corn cigar—the city's atmosphere was positively roiling around her. What was it all about? Why did it feel like it was adding up to something?

Standing there with her back against a wall, half of her brain was focused on the scene around her and the other half was searching for what she was supposed to be doing. She wasn't forgetful, she knew she was headed to the deli. She had her backpack strapped on, her wallet zipped into an inner pocket, she even knew exactly where her list was (left back pants pocket) and what was on it (garlic-stuffed olives, blue cheese, those very thin rosemary crackers, fresh pappardelle for her Friday night pasta extravaganza, roasted red peppers, and those Italian wedding cookies that she couldn't live without).

But she was stopped here on the corner of Broad and Chestnut Streets for a reason, she was sure of it. She felt like a big hand had pushed her up against the wall and made her wait there. What was she waiting for? A sign, a message, a gift?

Joelle. It was Joelle walking down the street right in front of her.

Geraldine roared Joelle's name out, she was so excited. She loved saying that name again after fifty years. It tasted so damn good in her mouth.

Joelle didn't turn around. Instead, she picked up her pace, throwing her canes out further in front of her and moving her braced legs forward in longer steps. Geraldine caught up with Joelle and stood in front of her, blocking her from moving.

"It's me, Geraldine. From Honeyman's. You remember."

Joelle's blue eyes were as blank as a mannequin's. Do I look that different at seventy-five than I did at twenty-five? Geraldine wondered. She still had the same men's haircut that the other office girls had teased her about, but now she wasn't afraid to wear men's clothes that fit her blocky body better than women's clothes ever had and construction worker boots that made her feel powerful when she walked the city streets, high-stepping over potholes and stomping up subway steps. Her hair was gray and her face had more wrinkles now, sure, but would that make her unrecognizable to Joelle? It didn't seem possible.

Joelle had aged very well. She still had that blonde flip, she still drew attention to her full mouth with red lipstick, and she still had the muscled upper arms of the dedicated swimmer she'd been back in her twenties. She even still smelled of Tabu, that scent Geraldine would hold inside herself after being near Joelle. Talk about intoxication. That woman was the whole package to Geraldine.

"Do you still swim? You look wonderful. I walk everywhere. That's how I stay fit. I can't believe I haven't seen you in fifty years. Honeyman's is long gone. The building was even demolished, did you know that? Luxury condos or some crap. Look at us. Wow. Look at you." Geraldine heard herself babbling but she couldn't seem to stop.

Joelle stepped back, held her cane high up in the air, and got into the cab that pulled over for her. She didn't even look back. Geraldine felt like Joelle had punched her in the stomach. Well, she'd show her. She waved at the next cab and told it to follow Joelle's, which was inching along in a traffic jam from street construction, lucky for her. Finally she saw Joelle get out of the cab in Old City and disappear down an alley off Chestnut Street.

Geraldine peeked around the corner to see Joelle seated at a small table across from an impossibly thin woman with gold front teeth. Geraldine waited for her breathing to slow down and her heart to stop rattling around in her ribcage. When she finally walked down the alley, she saw that the woman and Joelle were bent over tarot cards on the table, which also held a hand-written sign: *Psychic Reddings.*

The woman grinned up at her. Showing off her fancy teeth, Geraldine figured.

"Why'd you run away from me, Joelle? I only wanted to talk to you. It's been so long." Geraldine fought the urge to lean down and put her cheek next to Joelle's, skin to skin.

"I am not Joelle. You leave me alone." Joelle's voice was quavery but she sounded furious at the same time.

"But you are Joelle. I know you." Geraldine added it all up quickly in her mind: the blonde flip, the red lipstick, the chiseled upper arms, Tabu, the canes and leg braces from her childhood bout with polio. It was impossible that she was anyone else, she had to be Joelle.

"I said I'm not Joelle. If you don't stop following me and harassing me, I'll call the police."

Geraldine stayed put. This was Joelle, the first and only woman she'd ever loved. She had never told Joelle that she loved her, but she had tried to show her, daily leaving tomatoes, Chiclets gum, unsigned romantic cards (in case one of the others got nosy), lemon drops, and once even a ticket to the Phillies home opener on her desk. Geraldine had showed up at the baseball stadium, so nervous she was shaking, but Joelle hadn't. It would have been their very first date.

"This isn't fair," Geraldine cried out.

Joelle stood up so abruptly that the table fell over, sliding all the tarot cards onto the cobblestones. The psychic laughed like it was a good surprise. Geraldine watched Joelle walk away shaking her head.

Joelle could not have forgotten meeting Geraldine on the back stairs at Honeyman's during break time, the way they grabbed at each other and kissed greedily until Geraldine's mouth was covered in lipstick too, the feel of their bodies arched against the stairwell wall, listening for footsteps over their own panting breaths.

"You're right about her," the psychic said. "She told me first thing her name is Joelle from Jersey."

"I knew it," Geraldine said. "But why won't she talk to me? Why is she running away?"

There was the time Geraldine had to run down the steps and hide on the lower landing when the stairwell door burst open unexpectedly as she was unbuttoning Joelle's shirt. But she hadn't run away from Joelle, she'd never run away from her. Joelle told the co-worker who almost caught them together that day an elaborate story about hiding in the stairwell to cry, to explain her disheveled appearance. Geraldine had laughed the whole thing off, but Joelle had been so upset she'd gone home sick and not come back for days.

"I can answer that for you. It's all in the cards. Pick them up for me please, sister. Then shuffle them until you feel that you want to put them down. Do you have cash?" The psychic patted a small beaded purse hanging from her neck.

Geraldine had never had her tarot cards read before. It turned out to be a dizzying experience, the psychic slapping cards down fast, pointing at them, launching into long unintelligible explanations about what the cards signified, nothing that Geraldine could follow. The psychic sometimes looked up at the sky as if she was searching for answers and sometimes she broke into shrieking laughter as if she was hearing secret jokes whispered into her ears.

"Stop," Geraldine said finally. "I don't know what the heck you're talking about."

"Your life," the psychic explained. "I'm talking about you, sweetie." She pointed to the cards' positions. "This is you at this moment, what crosses you, what lies below you, what is swirling around you, your greatest hope, your greatest fear, what lies ahead of you. And here's your you-est you."

It was still gibberish to Geraldine. She got up to go, pulling money out to leave on the table. The psychic didn't really deserve it but Geraldine didn't want to stiff her. She'd never disrespect a woman worker.

"Wait," the psychic said. "Let's start over. Give me your palm, my dear."

"What for?" Geraldine didn't want to hold out her palm out to a stranger. That felt too vulnerable, too open, when all she wanted to do was close up and cry. When she was a kid in Catholic school, the nuns used to make them hold out their palms for small offenses and then smash down at them with metal-edged rulers, causing searing pain she'd never forgotten.

The psychic waited, her bony hand extended.

Geraldine sat down, stuck out her left palm, and started to cry. She felt like a fool. But Joelle had appeared in front of her like a dream come true and then she'd acted so mean and disappeared on her again. That was something to cry about.

The psychic pulled out a flask from under the table. Geraldine didn't even ask what it was, she didn't care. She drank one-handed until she felt warmth all the way down to her toes. She didn't know why alcohol had such a bad reputation when damn, it made life so much better. The psychic kept hold of her hand.

"Whew. Thank you for that," Geraldine said.

"You're a very needy woman," the psychic said. "You don't admit it, but you are." She closed her eyes and traced the lines in Geraldine's left palm.

That light touch on her palm felt as good as an orgasm to Geraldine. She hadn't been touched by another human being for a very long time now. Her palm was sending off little explosions of pleasure throughout her body. She moaned into the quiet air of the alley.

"Forget about Joelle, she's from your past," the psychic said. "I'm going to give you a look into your future."

Geraldine pictured Joelle walking back into the Honeyman building. She saw the building implode, the brick walls collapse, the dust cloud rise overhead. She saw files burning, papers flaming up and blowing away as ash. She saw the windows disappear, the big front doors vaporize, the stairwells cave in.

The psychic pulled both of Geraldine's hands toward her, palms up. Her fingertips roamed all over each of Geraldine's fingers, always circling back to the nerve centers in her palms. Geraldine's pleasure doubled, tripled, rippled everywhere in her body. Tears ran down her cheeks, she couldn't seem to control the flow.

"Oh baby, don't cry," the psychic said. "I see so much beauty and joy ahead for you."

"Really?" Geraldine couldn't believe it but she wanted to.

"What I see is a woman in love with her life, a woman whose life is full of pleasure. Not big thrills, not roller coaster excitement, but many small everyday joys."

"You got my number, all right," Geraldine admitted. She felt proud to be recognized. She often wondered why so many people didn't seem to understand how the little pleasures of life added up to big wonderful days.

Her friend Sumi used to say she'd done nothing with her day but when Geraldine pressed for more, she'd list a long litany of things that Geraldine considered the important things in life: making a tasty meal, a conversation with a friend, roaming around the city on fun little errands, an overheard sweet moment on a bus, a glass of wine on the front stoop, even picking up litter so their block looked pretty. You were so busy today, Sumi, Geraldine would tease her. Don't give me that nothing crap. Sumi would laugh and pretend to smack her. Geraldine missed Sumi every day.

"You're going to live a good long time," the psychic said. "And you'll be blissfully happy all the days of your life."

That sounded like hogwash to Geraldine. No one was blissfully happy all the time. Moderately happy most of the time was what she aimed for.

"But what about Joelle? Will I ever see her again?"

"Let's get real, sweetheart," the psychic snorted. "What did you really feel when you saw her again?"

Geraldine considered the strange episodes happening around her when she saw Joelle, the feeling that the universe had whipped up the city right then and held her against a wall until she could look Joelle in the eyes again after fifty years.

"Like I was dropped into a wormhole," Geraldine said. "Sent back in time to see the first woman I was crazy about, the woman I never forgot."

The psychic tapped a card. "Your past. That's all she was. This card is proof that she is out of your life."

"But why the hell did she appear in front of me today?"

The psychic put her forehead down on the table, resting on the Celtic Cross pattern she'd made with the cards. Was this part of the *psychic redding*? Geraldine wondered. She hated misspelled words. That alone should have warned her off this situation.

Something whizzed by Geraldine's head. She turned to see Joelle in the entrance of the alley holding a bag of baseballs. Joelle threw another ball closer to her this time; Geraldine swatted it away just before it hit her. The psychic raised her head to watch.

"Those are from the dollar store on the corner," the psychic said. "I'd know those balls anywhere."

"You're acting crazy, Joelle," Geraldine shouted. "Put the baseballs down."

Joelle reached into the bag and wound up for another throw. Geraldine and the psychic were sitting ducks in this dead-end alley full of dumpsters.

Geraldine looked around. She saw nothing she could use for a bat or a glove. Would the card table work as a shield? She shoved it over and held it in front of her, advancing down the alley toward Joelle like an Amazonian woman warrior. BAM, another ball smashed into the table hard. Geraldine felt the blow right in her breasts.

"I hate my future," Joelle screamed. "You're an awful psychic."

"What about me, Joelle?" Geraldine dropped the table so she could see her.

"I hate you too. You wrecked my life."

"What did I do?" Geraldine threw her hands up in the air. She really didn't know. In her memory, they'd never had a break-up fight, Joelle had simply not shown up to work one Monday, and from that day on had never called her back or opened her door to Geraldine again. She'd written many letters and cards pleading with Joelle, but she'd written *Return to Sender* on them and sent them right back unopened.

"I had to quit that job because of you," Joelle said. "I had to move back to stinking New Jersey."

"I thought we were in love," Geraldine said. The psychic looked surprised. She turned her head from Joelle to Geraldine again and again, like a dog shaking its head after being sprayed with water unexpectedly.

"Love," Joelle screamed. "The two of us weren't in love. You were chasing me, trying to lure me into your sick life. I was not going to be in love with you. I got married. To a man. I have kids, grandkids. Like a normal person. You're a freak. So there." She aimed at Geraldine's head and flung another ball. Geraldine ducked.

"All right, that's it," the psychic shouted, standing up and shaking her fist at Joelle. "No hate in my alley. Get out of here right now, you jerkwad dirtbag asshat."

Joelle hurled one last ball right at the psychic. Geraldine caught the ball with her bare hand just before it could hit the psychic in her gold-toothed mouth. It stung her palm like hell but she held it up in the air triumphantly, howling with delight.

In the many years that followed, that dollar-store ball sat on top of the small mantelpiece in Geraldine's living room as if it were a funeral urn full of ashes. It was the last object Geraldine had that was touched by Joelle; she would never let that go.

WILD AND FRAIL AND BEAUTIFUL

Candace Walsh

Cento, source: *Jacob's Room* by Virginia Woolf

something which can never be conveyed

uneven white mists
queer movements
chequered darkness

something in the room

yellow blinds and pink blinds
pink and yellow lengths of paper roses

something that would see them through

a tremulous haze
an eighteenth-century rain

something about being sure

the oval tea-table
the mustard on the tablecloth

something flying fast

iridescent pigeons
cloudy future flocks
a peacock butterfly

something whispers

a collection of birds' eggs
green wineglasses

something must be said

violets for sale
the violet roots and the nettle roots

something silver on her arm

small smooth coins
sea glass in a saucer

something for them

the flamingo hours
the worn voices of clocks

something like selfishness

the pale blue envelope
the soft, swift syllables

something very wonderful   has happened

YOU LOOK SO GOOD IN YOUR COVERALLS.

nerissa tunnessen

muddy knees   from praying too hard on the ground
                    pews lined in cabbage rows
                    psalms spat through rainbow chard
                    made to hold mass for the peonies
                    sat in strange soil

i see you kneeling: hands on the ground
wet earth parts her thighs for you
                              grass thighs
                              mulch thighs
                              thighs of weeds
                              dandelion and
                              yarrow and
                              plantain
you thrust
fingers deep in earth
sinking through her layers,
soft penetration with forefinger middle finger
gently easing in garlic cloves
back bent shovel hands
my strawberry baby plants
something sprouting
                    she brings together life as you touch her

two fingers part earth.
describe to me the feeling:
soft dirt on the pads of your fingertips
wet soil soaking your pant legs
                cool and soft, clinging to fabric capillaries to make her

way towards your thighs all slow in grit of jean
moisture towards petals in bloom

press in your knuckles.
  (can you feel the ground on your palms?
    does the grass lick your thighs your palms and—
    she pulls your hands deeper into her depths
    to feel her groundwater
    to feel her heartbeat
    to feel her to feel her to feel her—)

your first is hot around
garlic bulbs
sprouting from a single clove
multiplying
  movement-like
  delicious space invader
  community maker
  symbiotic product like
barriers coming together around dispersing
primary clove
shield of soft bulb

when i pull her from the ground in the spring
ill let you peel her layers from her
a new clove in your hand
a new clove in mine
you'll place her, nude, on the tip of my tongue
  let me curl her into my mouth,
    ease her down my throat
      pull your fingers into my mouth
        and kiss you, her sharp musk on my breath.

BUNNY & WOLF

Deanna Armenti

Howl & purr

i purr at you,
my Lover,
with passion,
the way a small bunny
purrs at the sun's warmth.

you howl at me,
your Lover,
with passion,
the way a Wolf
howls at their moon.

The bunny Cries Wolf

And the bunny
cries wolf,
Wolf, Wolf,
my Wolf...
out into the open sea
hoping the waves will
carry her small voice
all the way home
and sneak their way
through the forest [city]
up the tree [stairs]
into the burrow [room]
to whisper in Wolf's ear
Wolf, Wolf,
my Wolf

my heart is
always with you,
always yours.

Wolf's Teeth

Wolf flashes their perfect side smile the left side of their lip raised
in the most handsome grin

bunny counts each
of wolf's teeth
What nice teeth you have, bunny admires.

bunny admires everything about Wolf. bunny admires the
cowlicked fur [hair]
on their back [head]
and the eye of their tooth [heart] but especially the light in their
smile, the softness of their breath
on bunny furry tuft [neck]
as their side smile becomes a kiss.

Wolf's Smell

bunny skips across
the wooden path [boardwalk] paying close attention
to where earth has
started to reclaim
humankind's fingerprints
and thinks about how
Wolf smells like sand
and the earth's breath.

A New World

my wolf,
my protector,

i want to burrow next to you, make a home together with you and
hide away from
the rest of the world
for all of winter
and emerge
into summer's glow
starlings singing all around us, sun streaming, warming us
moss under our paws,
flowers dancing with us,
welcoming us
into a new world
of our own creation

HOW YOUR MOTHER BECAME THE GRASS

Monica Barron

Above all she knew grass—
the ways its leaves are green blades
released by their jointed stems with a boing
you can hear if the wind is not roaring
into the small, white faces of the flowers
waiting for pollen on the windward side
of a rolling hill. She knew herbage.

Your mother was a wild one, Billy—
a-bottle-of-vodka-in-the-freezer, a-shotgun-
behind-the-door kind of woman I couldn't
keep up with. She raised you to be a prairie child
who skis his way from Veterans' Day to Easter
in a fur-lined hat untroubled by clouds moving
faster than Red River of the North.

She came back to the Chariton River farm
when she knew her mother was dying.
They'd go to the pool and your mom would hold
her own mom, one hand under her neck, one
under the small of her back while she seemed to dissolve.

So don't you imagine, when she found herself
alone in the pasture having a heart attack,
she would fall in the blooming clover and Posy
would be there and the clouds would churn overhead
like pumping hearts until she became the grass.

THE LENS OF ETERNITY:
LESBIAN LOVE FROM TWO PANDEMICS

Janet Mason

And so, the days, as they are wont to do, wore on. Berenice Abbott's position ended at the end of the decade when the Works Progress Administration was disbanded at the end of the 1930s.

A few years earlier, Berenice and her long-time partner Elizabeth McCausland had lobbied for continued funding for the WPA and the Federal Arts Project (which was under the WPA, and which employed Berenice among others). Elizabeth, a journalist and the writer of the text of books that contained Berenice's photographs, wrote in the *Nation*:

"The Renaissance lasted three centuries, the Age of Pericles and the Augustan Age each half a century; for the 'cultural birth of a nation' our government allows less than two years."

Nonetheless, a few years later, at the end of the decade of the thirties, a new Congress voted down a bill that would've provided permanent funding and existing funding ran dry."

Berenice's days of hanging on rickety fire escapes and out of windows (regardless of how much she had loved them) to get the photograph were over.

Berenice survived the influenza pandemic in 1918 when she lived in Greenwich Village in Manhattan. Then she lived in Paris where she became a photographer and gained a reputation as a master of the craft. In Paris, she also met the older photographer Eugene Atget and when he died in 1927, she bought most of his archive and returned to live in Manhattan where she intended to sell the archive. She also returned because she was disillusioned with the café society in Paris and nostalgic for the United States. Berenice returned to live in Manhattan in 1929. In six years, in 1935, she met Elizabeth. After a whirlwind long-distance courtship, the two of them were together for three decades until Elizabeth's death when she was sixty-five. Berenice, who lived into her nineties and was to experience "success" in the form of fame and relative fortune for the first time at age seventy, then moved to the wilds of Maine for the last part of her life after the death of her long-time partner, Elizabeth.

Despite Berenice and Elizabeth being sickly all their lives, they kept on going.

Thanks to the Works Progress Administration, Berenice survived the Great Depression by finding work with the government for photographing and documenting the country during this era. And thanks to Berenice, the grand buildings of New York City in the 1930s had been preserved in her photographs for posterity.

As part of her New York City photographs (funded by the Works Progress Administration), Berenice photographed Pennsylvania Station in 1936. My first impression when I viewed the photograph titled simply "Pennsylvania Station" was that of the grandeur of light, simplicity, and beauty. Before it was demolished and "renovated," Pennsylvania Station was a work of art. High airy arches — a lattice of steel and glass — let in the light connecting the terminal to the heavens. In the photograph, the natural light filtered down to the circular illuminated face of a towering old-fashioned clock that looked like a grandfather clock made of stone. Clusters of globe lights lit the way down the steep stairs to the train platforms. Pennsylvania Station was torn down and remodeled in 1963. Since then, the station was almost all underground and it was remarkably unattractive. Berenice called its remodeling a "wicked" act.

When Berenice was cut from her job, she said, "The WPA knocked New York out of me."

What that meant for Berenice – at least temporarily – was that she was done photographing New York.

What that meant for the rest of us was that there were no more Berenice Abbott photographs of Manhattan until a decade later when Berenice found a publisher for a book of her photographs about her neighborhood. *Greenwich Village Today and Yesterday* was published in 1949 by Harper & Brothers (now an imprint of HarperCollins).

At the end of the thirties, when funding ran dry from the WPA, and with her fortieth birthday approaching, Berenice reinvented herself.

Berenice Abbott was, perhaps, best known for her photographs of New York City. Many knew her as the photographer who did *Changing New York* and who lived in Paris in the twenties and got her start as Man Ray's photographic assistant.

Berenice printed her own photographs into her mid-eighties. That she was so diligent in her work of printing in the darkroom (the importance of which she imparted to her students), no doubt contributed to her success and is something that could be traced back to her work assisting Man Ray.

All her life, Berenice took herself and her discipline seriously.

As Hank O'Neal says in *Berenice Abbott American Photographer* (a book of Berenice's photographs published in 1982 by McGraw Hill with text approved by Berenice when she was in her mid-eighties. Hank, who was a close friend of Berenice's, writes, "She does not regard one part of her work as any more significant than another, and she feels that sentimental judgments based on nostalgia miss the point altogether. Her point was graphically to capture the times – to make a record, in as artistic a fashion as possible, that would be of use to historians, sociologists and even art critics."

But things weren't over yet.

Both she and Elizabeth were drawn to science. Berenice knew that science was important. After all, penicillin was first developed in 1928, ten years after she nearly died in the influenza pandemic. A flu vaccine was under development and would be approved for first military and then civilian use in the mid-1940s. She thought that science would touch ordinary people's lives and change society for the better. But the average person needed to be taught to understand the concepts. They needed to learn from the photographs that she could take.

She maintained her opinion that photography was more of a science than an art. Even if she had wanted to be considered a fine art photographer, she had made it impossible to fit into that world when she insulted Stieglitz and Steichen in public by using the term "cult." She did this in 1951 when she spoke at a major photographic conference in Aspen, Colorado, and talked about the "cult" of photography led by Alfred Stieglitz (whose name was synonymous with fine-art photography) and his disciple Edward Steichen.

Berenice insisted that she didn't want to be considered an artist. She said that she disdained art and vehemently claimed that anytime she caught herself trying to be artistic, she ripped up the photograph.

In the 1930s, when Berenice returned to New York from her decade of living abroad, mostly in Paris, she saw Alfred Stieglitz by appointment to show him Atget's photographs, which she assumed he would be interested in. He bad-mouthed the photographer whose work he was exhibiting and then showed Berenice some of his own photographs which Berenice was not impressed with. He was not interested in Eugene Atget's work. (Berenice finally placed Atget's archive with the Museum of Modern Art in New York City when she was in her seventies – some fifty years after she had returned to living in the United States with the goal of placing his work. Atget finally entered history as a great pioneer and master of documentary and fine art photography.

As Berenice later told Hank O'Neal (as he writes in *Berenice Abbott American Photographer*):

"I felt there was something negative about the man (Alfred Stieglitz), Spiritual America was not of the low breed he had described. To judge America by European standards is foolish and a mistake. There was a new urgency here, for better or worse.

America had new needs and new results. There was poetry in our crazy gadgets, our tools, our architecture. They were our poems, and Hart Crane, perhaps our finest poet, recognized this. Stieglitz did not recognize it."

Undoubtedly, she had known many artists in Paris and must have continued to encounter artists — using the mediums of photography as well as paint — in her American circles of colleagues and friends. Her partner was an art critic. Considering that Berenice was known to be temperamental and to be a complainer, her objection to art may just have been a case of her own flaws writ large in others. On the other hand, her temperamental and complaining nature most likely would have been described differently if she had been a male photographer of a similar stature. Then her temperamental and complaining nature would just have been shrugged off as characteristic of someone who had high standards.

In any event, Berenice had long thought highly of science.

"'Essentially ours is a scientific age, rather than an artistic one,'" she would say quoting Leo Stein (the art collector and promoter as well as the older brother of the noted author Gertrude Stein) whom she had met in passing in the twenties in Paris. Obviously, his statement made a lasting impression on her.

Science was Berenice's next frontier. But she was turned down by most of the institutions she approached. The illustrations they already had of scientific concepts were fine, they said. But perhaps they were wrong. Considering the political divide, we'd come to in 2020 where half the nation believed in science and the other half denied it (or supported those in power who denied it), then it probably would have made a difference if Berenice's talents were put to use earlier.

This new frontier presented an uphill battle. As Hank O'Neal writes in *Berenice Abbott American Photographer*, *"Changing New York* had been a ten-year struggle. What Abbott did not know at the time was that her decision faithfully to photograph science, to attempt to link science and art, would involve her in a much more difficult struggle, which would take twice as long even partially to complete. In choosing science as a subject, she would soon find herself at odds with virtually everything that was in fashion in photography."

Her talents weren't put to work earlier – at least not full-time.

But there was free-lance work to be found.

And still, she persisted.

UNTITLED

Abby Wallach

```
               d        idn't
                 y        ou once say
                   k    nowledge is
          memor    y
          or ma    y      be that's just
     what i wante  d
        to thin    k
          you      k    now?
            b        e  cause
            i r        e   member
          ever   y        thing
                        e  ven though i
        wasn't     y   e  t
        i was b        e   fore
        memor      y
            an  d
            the    y
            ar        e
                   d   e  ad
        but not     y   e  t
            aft        e  r
        memor      y
          you      k    now what
            i m        e  an
                       e  verything
               is  d        iffer-
                       e  nt
            b          e  cause
          the    y
```

```
ar        e  n't
   h      e  re
an  d
   b      e  -
caus      e
  the  y
   ar     e
              s
  an  d
   b      e
caus      e
i am
```

TRINITY

Abby Wallach

remember that there is strength in protecting this body / the ruched white lines + this censored blood + my bones / beneath it all, the fury / not this jagged edge but rather the mouth that i may speak you through / & i remind myself that this is all i was made for / to exist, to bear witness, to fall in love each day with each evolving sunset / remember this mirrored face, those two wondering eyes / are my instrument.

---

armed with rage as fundamental as my reborn skin / i returned in the second movement of midnight to the freedom of a stranger's home / the slow sobs in the upstairs hall the curse of another mother's son / my fist a rogue soldier & my own face the closest criminal / as if my stifled shout was the world's fiercest shriek / as if my starvation ends the moment my twisted smile shatters / and for what? / for the softer disappointment filigreed across my mother's face? / for the moment before the mirror transforms when we are nothing at all?

---

we born into anger duller and deeper than hatred / we who were lovers in the crevices and spouses in the pastel-perfect houses / we whose shouts were heard around the world / the resonance of the brick-shattered windows still echoing past our overgrown graves / we the bloodied with our howls hysterical / aching tongues flapping in the crushing quiet of our ghost-towns / we a nation flatlining / our pulse a thousand swallowed screams / we: marsha + harvey + matthew + the decimated millions + uncountably more / we who were never allowed to survive / whose deaths must not equal our silence we born into anger duller and deeper than hatred / remember that there is strength in protecting this body / armed with rage as fundamental as my reborn skin / i returned in the second movement of midnight to the freedom of a stranger's home / we who were lovers in the crevices and spouses in the pastel-perfect houses / we whose shouts were heard around the world / the ruched white lines + this censored blood + my bones / the slow sobs in the upstairs hall the curse of another mother's son / the resonance of the brick-shattered windows still echoing past our overgrown graves / beneath it all, the fury / my fist a rogue soldier & my own face the closest criminal / we the bloodied with our howls hysterical / as if my stifled shout was the world's fiercest shriek / not this jagged edge but rather the mouth that i may speak you through / aching tongues flapping in the crushing quiet of our ghost-towns / we a nation flatlining / & i remind myself that this is all i was made for / as if my starvation ends the moment my twisted smile shatters / our pulse a thousand swallowed screams / and for what? / to exist, to bear witness, to fall in love each day with each evolving sunset / for the softer disappointment filigreed across my mother's face? / we: marsha + harvey + matthew + the decimated millions + uncountably more / remember this mirrored face, those two wondering eyes / for the moment before the mirror transforms when we are nothing at all? / we who were never allowed to survive / are my instrument / whose deaths must not equal our silence

SHANGHAI NIGHTS

S. C. Gordon

It was mid-afternoon when the doorbell rang, in that idle hour after three o'clock, between the flurries of mealtimes, before the schools let out. I hadn't been expecting guests but often a student or friend would drop by after lunch to borrow a book or drink tea in the garden. I had a basement flat in a Georgian terrace off the Old Brompton Road; my little trellised yard made me a popular prospect in the summertime.

When I opened the door there was a young man standing at the bottom of the steps. He looked about twenty-five – old enough to be working but too clean-faced to have married yet. He wore a white shirt open at the collar, dust-red trousers, and beige deck shoes with messy leather laces. A lock of pale hair grazed his eyebrows.

"Good afternoon," I said.

"Oh, good afternoon."

His voice was proud but careful. From those three words I guessed his provenance: a good school, a boisterous family of brothers, a wealthy father and a nervous mother who was happier in the countryside.

"Pardon me for disturbing you," he said. "But are you Miss Milne?"

"I am."

"Miss Victoria Milne?"

"Vicky to my friends, although we aren't yet, are we?"

The shift in my stance was proof of my impatience. It made him stand up straighter.

"I'm Ed," he said.

"Hello, Ed."

Such a blunt name, like a doorstop or a block of cheese.

"Ed Moreau," he said.

My vision suddenly contracted like a zoom lens. "Oh, I see."

He lowered his head a little, but not his gaze.

"I believe you knew my great-aunt Monica."

It had been so long since I'd heard her name spoken aloud that for a moment I was speechless. I sensed more keenly the hum of the bees in the wisteria that grew around the door. I smelled the fug of distant traffic and felt the texture of the sun on the silk scarf I'd wrapped my hair in so I didn't have to wash it.

And then I laughed. I laughed for the relief of it, of knowing I hadn't imagined it after all; that there had, indeed, been a Monica Moreau who breathed and lived and walked the earth.

"I don't mean to intrude –" Ed said. He looked concerned, as if he suspected I was senile from the tone of my laughter.

"No, no. I'm delighted you're here. But how did you find me? That was all such a long time ago."

He brightened, bolstered by my levity, freed from the initial risk embedded in his mission.

"We have a mutual friend – Dr. Pargeter," he said.

"Sam, you mean?"

"Yes."

Immediately this connected us in a way more tangible than Monica.

"And how is he?" I asked.

"He's well," Ed said, then paused, unsure whether to toe this path and deepen our amity, or to press on. "Shanghai came up in conversation. Daddy mentioned that his aunt had lived there in the 1930s. My great-aunt. Dr. Pargeter didn't know her, but he gave us your name."

"How kind of him. And you're hoping I'll – what? Tell you all about her?"

"Well, yes." He gave an oddly unappealing little laugh. "You knew her, didn't you?"

"I did," I said, inclining my head with a wistfulness I thought would suit the moment. "Yes, I did."

"I'd like very much to hear about her," Ed said. "If it wouldn't trouble you."

Already it was clear I fit the bill. So far I hadn't disappointed him. With my gaudy turban, the cigarette in my hand, and what he could see of my home from the doorway – Chinese screens, dusty dried flowers in vases, legions of books on listing shelves – I was precisely what he'd expected from a friend of the long-lost black ewe of his clan.

I invited him in. When he passed me in the narrow porch the air turned with a mannish smell: cut grass, a slow game of cricket played earlier in the day, a faint reminder of the cologne he'd tapped onto his cheeks with flat palms in the bathroom mirror.

There was nothing of Monica in him at all. He was as pale and neat as a peeled boiled egg, where she had been all sultry brown and rangy – the trace of her Ceylonese grandmother, which had evidently been bred out before Ed's generation.

I tucked my cigarette into the nearest ashtray and led him into the kitchen. His pace slowed with mannered curiosity at the pictures on my walls, the cabinets and mirrors and coat stands – things I'd picked up along the way as the daughter of a diplomat. My father was dead now; he'd been gone ten years, but he was everywhere still, just as Monica was, several layers below.

"Tea?" I said.

"Please."

"You're not sick of the stuff?"

"Pardon me? Oh – I see. No. No, I'm not sick of it."

In his carefully controlled hesitancy I saw how he was when at ease – prone to laughter, amenable, with a sense of humour that wasn't quite sharp enough to be sarcastic.

"You're not in the family business, then?" I asked, pointing for him to sit down at the kitchen table while I laid the tea things out.

"I am, as it happens," he said. "Although we're a far more humble enterprise nowadays. Daddy has a boutique in Hampstead."

"Is that so?" I said, faintly charmed. "A boutique. I had no clue. Although it's not often I venture north."

"What do you do?" Ed asked in a dinner party voice.

"Many things," I said. "I teach the piano. I read books. Such a lot of them. And I have plenty of friends to pass the time with. It's a boon to come from wealth, as you'll know," I said. "It means not having to strive particularly hard at any one thing. Here, look —"

I had lifted down a canary-yellow tea caddy from the back of a cupboard. It was darkened with rust at the corners.

Ed took it. It looked much smaller in his hands. He eyed it, confused, still digesting my musings on money. It discomfits some people to talk openly of it.

Moreau & Co.
1936
Traders in fine tea
China, India, Ceylon

"This is marvellous," Ed said, holding it closer to his face. "I've never seen one in such good condition."

"Keep it," I said. "I have plenty of them. Put it in your shop window, for posterity."

"I couldn't possibly."

He was holding it like a rare fossil.

"You must," I said. "Or I'll be mortally offended."

"Thank you." He smiled, cautious with the first inklings of having gained the measure of me. "Daddy will be delighted."

"Your daddy is David's son, am I right?"

"Yes. David was my grandfather. Did you know him?"

"Yes, I did."

"I never met him. He died before I was born," Ed said with the practiced regret of inherited grief. "What was he like?"

I wrestled for the right words, determined to remain truthful while affording this young man a hero's memory of his grandsire.

"Strident," I said finally.

I busied myself filling the kettle, remembering my hand on Monica's dead hand at her bedside, then David's hand coming down from my shoulder to rest on my arm, not in sympathy or comfort – no – but to unclasp Mo's gold watch from my wrist and slide it into his pocket.

"And what was my great-aunt like?" Ed asked.

As he spoke I was caught unawares by a dismal tug at the back of my throat, like the warning tannoy beside the canal before the lock begins to fill. I ignored it. Four decades had passed since 1936. More. Four decades and four years. I could be frank without it setting me back. Nevertheless I lowered my voice.

"Ed, it is a very long story about a very short period of time, and I don't wish to bore you, but I will tell you – and I hope this won't strike you in any way as frightening or appalling – that everything you see here, everything about me, if you ever come to know me better, is a result of Momo."

His eyebrows lifted in a dumb smile.

"Is that what you called her?"

I nodded, deflated at his refusal to thank me in some way for my candour.

"How funny," he said. "I must remember to tell Daddy."

"Yes, you must."

I went to the stove so I wouldn't have to watch him turning the canary-yellow caddy over in his hands, – *Moreau & Co. Traders in fine tea* – lolling in my kitchen chair, flushed with summer, happy to have this quaint nugget of family history to share at his dinner parties.

"It's a pity she died so young," he said at the end of a yawn.

I stared down at the tealeaves spinning in the pot and made a grim noise of agreement.

"How old was she, exactly, when she passed?"

"Forty," I said.

"My... That's no age, is it? Even back then. And how old was she when you met her?"

"Forty."

I heard the feet of his chair touch the floor. He must have been leaning back.

"Gosh, then you barely knew her at all."

I turned and placed the teapot down on the table with all the fortitude I could muster.

"I'd say it really isn't up to you, Ed, to speculate like that."

He shrugged his shoulders equably, childishly, and I wanted to shove the teapot into his lap for his unwillingness to see me as anything more than a cipher in his tepid investigations.

"I don't suppose you have any pictures of her," he said "Or any of her things?"

"Not much," I said. "Your grandfather saw to it that her worldly goods were taken care of. And the rest of her."

Ed sat up straighter.

"Oh – I've visited her grave."

"Her grave?"

Even after all these years there were words I still found impossible to associate with Mo. *Her death. Her funeral.* And now *her grave.*

"Yes," Ed said, happy that the tables were turned and he could offer me something. "It's just close to here, at the Brompton Cemetery."

It was the worst and most alarming thing he could possibly have said – the fact of Mo's bones lying just two streets away, when all this time I'd believed her to be on the other side of the world, in a damp corner of some treaty port columbarium. It was so desperately startling that it made me laugh. I shook with bright billows of black glee. Ed joined in, hesitantly at first, then heartily. It was so uniquely morbid as to be delicious.

"Didn't you know?" he said, keen for the moment to continue.

"I had no idea at all."

"Then you must visit. We'll go together sometime."

He mistook my subsiding chuckles for assent. In fact I had no desire to see him again, or his father, or their boutique in

Hampstead. At first it felt cruel to deprive them of a link to Mo, but I knew there would be no truth in it, in any case – in their idea of me as a mere passing acquaintance. I asked myself quickly if Mo would have held my reluctance against me. For all her bluster she'd possessed a charming sense of duty that made her love the folk she was supposed to, in spite of their flaws: her distant father, her venal brother and, it stood to reason, this pallid oaf of a great-nephew who was sitting in front of me. But as much as I tried, I couldn't countenance the idea of involving myself any further than this. To make up for it I offered to play Ed some songs on my old gramophone – two of Momo's favourites in particular.

"Yes, please," he said cheerfully, as if I'd suggested a steak pie or some such – one of the deeply ordinary pleasures I assumed he enjoyed.

"They're old Chinese songs," I said, hauling the contraption out of the cupboard. Ed made only a lame show of helping, raising a lazy inch off his chair but sitting back down straight away.

"Listen first, then I'll translate," I said.

"You know Chinese?"

"Of course."

I rummaged among the brittle record covers for the one I was looking for. It was close to the top of the pile; I listened to it every once in a while.

"I lived in many places in my youth," I said. "It always struck me as the least I could do to learn their languages."

"I speak French," Ed offered.

"Yes, I'm sure you do."

With the gramophone wound up I laid the record down and lowered the stylus. Then I sat to drink my tea while it played. It was a Zhou Xuan song, jumpy and bright below the scratchy overtones of age. Just one verse in and I was back at the cocktail bar at the Cathay Hotel, the memory of Momo's hair pinned with two opal combs, the dull and brutal pull of love, just as strong as it always had been.

"That's a fine tune," Ed said when it finished. "Quite jolly."

"Isn't it?"

"What's it about?"

He caught my eye over the rim of his teacup and seemed to regret asking; I hadn't changed my expression quickly enough.

"It goes like this," I said. "It goes *Shanghai nights, Shanghai nights. Lift the lanterns to the music of the streetcars –*"

"How lovely."

"*Let's sing and dance.*"

Ed looked pleased with himself, as if he'd finally settled on a satisfying image of his great-aunt, singing, dancing among the lanterns in a tableau of the Orient.

I carried on. "*Let's pretend we're still happy and rich…*"

His face fell.

"Is that what it says?"

"Yes."

"Well, that's rather depressing."

"Is it?" I said. "Why?"

He glowered. "Pretending to be happy and rich."

"Is it really so bad to pretend?"

He had nothing to say to that. He surely thought I was senile now, if he hadn't before.

Dear boy, I thought. *Just wait until life disappoints you so much that pretending is the cleanest option.*

We listened to the second song in silence – a mournful Bai Guang dirge with a trudging bass and wailing clarinets.

The darkening of my mood became apparent to Ed as the verses drew on. He fidgeted, and drained his teacup as if pre-empting a swift egress just as soon as politeness permitted.

"You'll find this one even more depressing," I said.

"Yes – I'm not sure I like it."

"Your great-aunt did. She liked it very much. It was her favourite."

Ed cleared his throat.

"I'll tell you what the words mean," I said. "That way you'll know us both a little better."

"There's no need, really. I oughtn't take up any more of your time. You've been very generous as it is."

"But I insist."

His cheeks had coloured. He was uncomfortable but I went on regardless.

"It means, more or less, this:" I held his gaze staunchly as I spoke, willing him to keep it, daring him to look away.

"*I'm waiting for you to come back. I want you to come back.*"

He blinked steadily.

"*Waiting makes me happy. Waiting means I still love you after all.*"

His jaw tightened.

"Beautiful, no?" I said. "Mo used to sing it to me, when we were to be apart. She went on trips, you see. To the plantations down at Yunnan. I sang it to her, as well. I still do, even. Still, sometimes."

Ed moved as if to rise.

"No, there's more," I said. "Listen. It only grows more beautiful."

His shoulders tensed but he obeyed.

"*Until you come back there'll be no springtime,*" I recited. "*Only hot tears on my cheeks.*"

He gave a prim cough. "Miss Milne..."

"The original Chinese is lovely here," I said. "'Hot tears' is *re lei.* Isn't that wonderful? *Re lei.* So haunting."

Ed stood up. "I really ought to be leaving. Thank you for your time. And for this." He tucked the caddy under his arm. *Moreau & Co. Traders in fine tea.*

I didn't stop him this time. I was listening to the last lines of the song as they faded.

The swallows have returned to the roof beam. Around the door, the flowers bloom to welcome you back.

The year I knew the Moreaus was the beginning of my life in earnest. I was twenty-one and new to Shanghai. Before, it had been one boarding school after another, the only difference being the view from the window – Nairobi, Bulawayo, Batavia, Lausanne.

I met Monica at an afternoon gala for expatriate wives. She wasn't like the rest of the women in their pale gowns and neat hair. She was wearing black velvet dress that was all wrong for the season, and a grim look that proved she didn't care, and had possibly selected it on purpose. I found myself standing beside her at the drinks trestle waiting for a fresh bowl of punch to be brought out.

"I oughtn't really be here, you know," she said in low tones. She was chewing something.

I glanced around to make sure she was, in fact, talking to me.

"No?"

"I'm not an expatriate wife, as such." She took a peach stone from her mouth and cast her eyes about for somewhere to discard it. Almost without thinking I held my empty punch glass out. The wizened stone, whiskered with yellow flesh, toppled in with a muted thwack.

She grinned at me.

"Thank you," she said. "You see, I'm actually –" She leaned to whisper in my ear. "An expatriate mistress."

"Oh…"

"At least, I was," she said with a bitter little frown that was purely for show. "But that's my expatriate's actual wife over there in the awful gingham skirt. So, possibly I shouldn't be here at all."

"Nor should I," I said. "If it's only for wives. I'm an expatriate's daughter."

"Are you?"

"My father is the new vice-consul."

"You poor thing. The diplomatic services are a bore, aren't they? I'll wager you haven't spent more than two years in a single place."

"Barely."

"Well, not to worry. You're of age now, I presume."

"Yes. Twenty-one. Just."

She beamed at me.

"Then you can go – or stay – where you please. How liberating."

I had met a lot of people in my life but none like her. She glowed with something – a vibrant commonality that made her seem at once wholly foreign and altogether familiar. She was the nameless and ineffable thing I had always wanted to be.

Her family sold tea to China, she told me. "Would you believe? Just as the saying goes. We're chancers, really. Mavericks." And they – her father and her brother, both named David – were a thousand times more witty and germane than my own dour tribe.

As often happened in expatriate circles we grew close quickly. She took me on with seasoned alacrity. She'd had dear friends before, she said, but none quite as fetching as me. What she meant, in fact, was *willing*. I did her bidding. I gave her all time she asked me for, sitting with her in cafés and walking with her among the frost-paled rockeries in the park. I listened, clucking with feigned understanding, to her rages and gripes about her former lover – a tycoon whose name I'd heard – which formed the basis of our earliest discussions. On observing her consummate social poise at the gatherings she took me to (parties at the Cathay, soirees at the clubs, *to show you what Shanghai is like*) I began to perceive the darling weaknesses she hid so well from other people.

She went with her brother and father almost weekly to tea plantations outside the city, to Wujing and Hangzhou, and as far afield as Fujian. It was in her absences that I first became aware that my fondness for her was sprawling in an uncharted direction. It was hotly confusing at first, but soon I grew wise of how to manage it even as it grew. I kept my own counsel. The agony of it was preferable to the scorn I would inevitably face if I admitted it. For months and months, the whole of the winter and spring, I said nothing when she took my hand or laid her head in my lap – the tender trappings of close friendship that I valued too desperately to forfeit.

At parties, if she wasn't by my side I watched her from across the room, following the line of her throat as she laughed in her typical wide-mouthed wonder at the world and all it offered.

With two decades more than me on her side, she schooled me on how to behave, what to do (*Whatever you choose, my dear. There's pleasure to be had in almost everything, if only you can weed it out*) and how to avoid the mistakes she had made – close calls with men she hadn't loved, falling too madly for people who weren't expecting it.

I was sure that in her words lay a prescribed certainty of our respective roles – she as the mentor and I as the ingénue. I accepted it, but as it happened, I was wrong.

One night in June we had left the French Club after a party. It was raining. The rain was a blizzard; the trees were full of it. We ran the two long blocks to the Moreau villa in our dripping finery, hand in hand. When we reached the gate she stopped short and turned. Out of step, I fell against her. She laughed and drew me in for our usual farewell embrace. But this time neither of us let go. Perhaps it was the wine we'd drunk, or the particular closeness of a whispered joke we'd shared. Whatever it was, it acted as a force that kept us face to face and blinking, both of us smiling a little ruefully at the fact of this never having happened before. When I kissed her the wetness of her mouth was different from the rain on her face. It brought a memory up unbidden, of a time in Kenya when I'd watched a bare-armed man slit the taut gullet of a goat, and its innards had spilled in a skein onto its sweating hide.

I wondered if she would less ebullient, less relentlessly joyful, in bed. *If you are*, I thought, *I think I shall never love anyone else.*

I woke the next morning to white sunlight. The trees outside had been cleansed and made greener by the rain.

There came a knock at the door and David as there, a straw fedora in his hands.

"Aren't you up yet?" he said. "We're to leave for Kunming in an hour."

He was talking to Mo but it was me he looked at. I held the bed sheet to my chin.

"Alright," Mo muttered beside me, still mostly asleep. "Yes, alright."

Before he stepped back into the hallway David eyed me darkly, sucked his teeth, and shook his head.

They were away for three weeks to oversee the harvest on the Moreau plantations in the south. There was a telephone at the hill station from which she called me every evening.

She caught malaria there. We didn't know for a month or two after they returned. It crept up slowly, weakening her spirit and sending her to sweating purdah in the back bedroom.

To my surprise, David allowed me to take care of her.

"It's only because she said she'd sooner die than be without you," he muttered to me one night at her bedside above the sick rasp of her sleeping breath. "Although I wonder if sooner wouldn't be better, for the bother of it all."

She died and it became me for a while – a layer of carbon paper that sat between me and anything I did. It was absurd. I'd known her hardly at all and still it ruled me for many years. Too many years.

After Ed left I cleared the teacups from the table and went to sit in the garden for a while. I wanted to recalibrate, to remind myself that I had breathed unceasingly since then, and would unceasingly until at last I didn't, whenever the day came for it. Living, it seemed, was the only thing that kept me living. It was comical, in its way, for its very surety.

I pulled the old gramophone out onto the filigree table and played the record again. I laughed to myself as the lyrics made true around me in the chatter of early summer. The swallows had returned to the roof beam. Around the door, the flowers bloomed to welcome her back.

A LESBIAN WITH A MEGAPHONE

Sarah Sarai

No one looks twice at
a lesbian with a megaphone.
Except us. We note
the curves of her learning.
We're keen on her narration
of our giddy march down
Fifth each year in Spring.
There's value to her learning.
There's value to her curves.
Precise with a power fueled
by right place—right time,
and thousands avowing love,
the drummers Lady Lesbian
floats behind are fierce as war.
DYKE DYKE DYKE DYKE
MARCH! Oh, they're on
Cloud Nine, over the moon,
walking on air, friendly with joy.
Our Lady of Lesbians calls
Join us! to the sidelines where
shills of Big Fear flash posters
warning some god'll disavow us.
Sure. Right. Some god that is.
Megaphone Lez' ladypart-
words take to the streets,
not to battle but to find a cafe.

SNOW ON THE ROOF

LauRose Felicity

My woman lover
Fucks me
Without a strap on
Entering me
Slow and deep
My breath hissing as she moves
In and out.
She says it's her energy.
And I believe.

My woman lover
Says she has never been named a Witch
But it seems to me
She's her own consecration
And a renewal of mine.
Majik running through her fingers,
Tracing spirals of desire
On my clit
Calling my
Eddies of orgasm that build
Like a long, long, wave
Of aching pleasure
Swelling my entire ocean till the crash.
All of me is carried on this flood.

My womon lover
Sings
In a voice
Rich as dark honey
And again,

High, and aching.
Listening
Like an eavesdropper
I glance away
I am starstruck
Too shy to meet her eyes,
But I am an avid fan.

With my woman lover,
In each
Of the minutes
Of Our first
13 day kiss
I have been
Awakened
And comforted
Heard
And shocked
Warmed
And alive.
And I would not relinquish one instant
Of this autumnal adventure.

For myself,
I'm an old woman
Grandmother
Silvered crone.
But as I was taught
In my Kentuckiana mountain family
"Snow on the roof don't mean there's no fire in the hearth

And this one
Is a full on blaze.

THE GREY BITCHES

LauRose Felicity

This old wolf's howl
Of sexual desire
Reverberates in your darkness
Breaking your feverish, restless sleep
You lie hearing
A pulse so long suppressed.
Thrumming.
Come out, I cry,
Come out.
Yes, it is dangerous and sometimes lonely here.
But so is unconsciousness.
Claim your kisses
Liquid on your lips
Flowing quickly
To your other opening.
Before your chances cease.
Women.
Find each other.
Unused bodies are more tragic
Than embarrassment
Or the mourning of a love's loss.
Because you are losing right now.
And will never find
Unless you come out,
And hunt
For ecstasy.

ODE TO BARBARA HAMMER

Alexandra Volgyesi

Double Strength (1978) at Company Gallery,
"Tell me there is a lesbian forever..." October 2021, NYC

1.

I watch you soaring across the sky like falcons. Playing or preying. And notice how close "preying" falls to "praying" on the ear— asking for mercy or asking for a meal. Hoping and demanding the world keep you alive.

You are powerful and tender. I see in the muscles moving under skin the birth of a new world — you, woman. Woman of steel or clay. The handiwork of carving the meaning of another lifeforce, another grammar into your cheek, so new language spills out of you. And you don't say a word. Your words are the camera falling onto a new breath, onto new skin. I see you and I see myself in a new angle. See your muscles I never knew I had. Can my arms move like this? Can my back muscles bear the strength of all it carries — you pull yourself up and I see oars rising, pushing the hull through mountainous waves, crashing against your back.

You are beautiful in a language I've never heard before. But I see it, now. I see you smile the sun of a maple tree's morning. The bark of your smile rough and earthy. Rough as in unruly, as in refusing the ordered cruelty of the world to bend you into its shape. You allow yourself to be weathered by wonder. By the joys of life, I see it on your skin. I see how joy has carved rivers by your eyes. And maybe there is a god, because in woman I see the songs of the starlit desert. I see the etchings of water running across the earth to impart upon us life. You run across the floor and I feel the rock of the earth beneath your feet becoming part of each step, transforming your body into the mineral that made us.

2.

I leave the gallery, but your film is still running. The squares of film unfurl against the buildings in staccato, and I see the Bowery Kate fell in love with. In it are the ghosts of my own youth's wonders — the life I made with strangers in the anarchy basements of Budapest, Aurora, the feminist library. Where I read "Lesbian/Woman," with the light beaming in and the whole world felt connected. Where we ate corn the elderly woman cooked us and C seasoned it the way they do in Colorado, and we were growing stronger from the corn and nourished with knowledge and energy.

I discovered lesbian politics and came to life.   I was alive — I was the morning sun
casting itself across the glinting ice caps of
mountains. I was the marmots peeking out from against rock, the gentle ebb of the lake brushing against the
mountain lilies. I was the blades of grass basking under the warmth as the sun inched up and threw itself against the whole of the valley.

Reaching, reaching, and the burst of energy and life in the overwhelming warmth. Tell me god isn't a woman. So happy I could cry, and we happily chewed our corn. The
memory floods back to me with the warmth of a valley. With the breeze of a
mountain lily beside a lake. Gentle paddle of waves against the rocks.

This is the light I see against the buildings in their film reels, until they redden and burn into a liquid and fall away. I try to look for them. I scour the buildings for a sign of the past I could taste on my tongue. I know this feeling — I've felt it. It was just here! Where did it go? Kate and Vita, they were just here. They had just left a meeting and they were discussing the revolution. I was here with them. I was learning all about the ways to make the world the light and the trees and the grass it was always meant to.

Where are they? Haven't I come to the city to find them? To relive the joys of a land I can't go back to, anymore. The world I lived in has changed and I won't find it again. I've doven into the archives and realistically, these things only last a few years before burning into a light it can't contain. It melts and falls away to reveal the cruel order it was trying to cover up.

               You can't change things. You can't change a world
                  invested in its own death. That finds feverish
                      pleasure in its destruction.

Let me find them, again!

Let me run away into the forest and the sun and emerge with the energy of a hundred voices chanting the same future. Let me feel the valley of my body cloaked in the warmth of a hope and a joy that can only be god. Let me cry with the relief of a found religion. Let me fall against the ground and feel against me the mineral of my own body and the earth at once. I will find them again. Barbara, you've helped build a world, and I won't let them destroy it. Won't let your language be cruelly twisted into a eulogy. Your life force into a damnation. It is the trick of the wicked to convince the world of light's danger, and I see that now. You demand a life that was to be taken from you. In the sharpness of a falcon's beak is the wanting of a world that knows only mercy. You want from the world only what you can take and still preserve it. Life is not death, including a mutilating self-sacrifice we've been taught to cherish. The joining in of putting out the light of the world to clamor for what little sun we can grasp and call it bounty. But you've taught me love is abundant, because this world is limitless.

3.

You fly against the sky and I call you a miracle. You carry with you a light, deciding you would not allow yourself the death of a world forgotten.

AN INTERVIEW WITH SOUTHERN LESBIAN PLAYWRIGHT GWEN FLAGER: WRITING HISTORY ONTO THE STAGE NO MATTER HOW LONG IT TAKES

Elizabeth S. Gunn

Award-winning playwright Gwen Flager is a self-described southern lesbian and author of 10 original plays. Flager won the 2017 Queensbury Theatre's New Works playwriting competition for her original script, *Shakin' the Blue Flamingo* (formally titled *Girls Who Sing in the Choir* as an homage to *Boys in the Band*), premiering in 2018. Flager's additional plays were produced by the 2019 Santa Cruz Actors' Theatre 8 Tens @ 8 Festival, the 2017 Midwest Dramatists Conference, the 2015 Scriptwriters Houston10 x 10 Showcase, the 2012 Scriptwriters Houston Fifth Annual Museum Plays, and Theatre Suburbia 2010 season.

Flager's play *Shakin' the Blue Flamingo* is scheduled for production by Dirt Dogs Theater Co. at Match Theater in Houston, Texas, in August 2022.

This interview explores both Flager's identity as a southern lesbian author and her process of writing lesbian characters and content within the context contemporary United States theater. The conversation centers on the purpose and intentionality of her work as Flager reflects on her time as a young lesbian in the deep south in Louisiana and Alabama. She speaks to the process of becoming a playwright, and she considers the stories of strong women, many of whom are lesbians, who all too often remain marginalized in both history and theater. Layered into the interview are references from Flager's work and life to southern cuisine, family secrets, racism, gossip, hidden matriarchs, unmarried sex and childbirth, the open secret, and destabilizing heteronormativity hinged on fault lines of the façade of religious superiority.

This interview was recorded on Thursday, February 10, 2022, in Henderson, Nevada, at Flager's home in the warm afternoon breeze on her back porch. Present for the interview were her two small, friendly dogs, Izzy and Maggie. The interview has been edited for clarity. Many thanks to Flager for her generosity of time and spirit in meeting and corresponding about her work. Thank you as well to Flager's wife Ruthann Adam for sharing her home for the purpose of this interview.

Tell me about the first time it occurred to you to write a play.

I had tried my hand at short stories and was apparently unsuccessful in getting recognition as it were. And then I thought well maybe I'm not very good. Maybe that's not what you need to be writing. I had taken a lot of little courses at Rice University's continuing studies for writing novels or short stories or different formats and decided that my best quality was dialogue. So, if you just started eliminating what you're not good at, well perhaps plays would be my best venue. I talked to a friend of mine about it and she knew of a fellow that could help. I had started a short story and I thought this might be something to develop into a play. It started out about a pin, about a young woman leaving home, leaving her grandmother's house. So, I started working with this gentleman who helped me with the first couple of drafts, and I decided that I could do this. It seemed the natural avenue to take.

What got you interested in writing that first short story?

Well, we had a wreck. My sister sent me an angel pin after the wreck. The car was totaled. So, that started my wanting to write a story about this pin. There's a side story about this pin. So, I started writing and wrote probably four or five pages. I can't remember if I showed it to anybody and they said, "hey, this might make a great play," or "why don't you develop it." It started with the dialogue and the story developed from there. I talked to a friend that works in film. She referred me to this fellow, and I showed it to him, and that's kind of how that story got started.

Was it something about the accident or the pin that prompted you to write?

The significance of the wreck. I was driving. The car was totaled. By the time everything came to a complete halt, we had been hit by three different vehicles and a bus. We went spinning like a top down the highway and wound up in the complete opposite direction when the car came to a stop. I thought I had killed Ruthann. And so, my sister sent me this angel pin. And a story resonated that maybe the only thing a young woman could take with her was an angel pin. The situation at home wasn't safe for whatever reason and she had to leave. Her grandmother said, "you keep this pin with you, it will protect you." And it morphed into a much longer story. And it turns out in the play that the pin's never referenced, and as the story developed, the young woman turned out to be a niece. The pin never appears in the play.

Which play is that?

Waiting to Be Mended. The very first one.

When you thought about doing something creative, how did you find writing versus other art forms?

I remember writing as a kid, and I never pursued it in college. I never took any writing courses. I never really did much with it other than in certain altered states, and the next morning I would wonder, "who wrote this, you can't even read this." I enjoyed writing, it was a good outlet, and I always felt like there were stories I needed to tell. Maybe not my stories, but other people's stories, like maybe I could tell their stories or tell the similarities in our stories. And I learned early on that not everyone can do that. I've had people say, "gosh, that's happened to me," or "I have an aunt or a sister or whoever like that." And there are people who just can't express what's important to them or what matters to them.

Having read all your plays, there is universality, but a lot if not all are set in the South.

Yes, I grew up in the South. I went to school in Mobile, which is really South, and you get much more South and you're in the Gulf of Mexico. And I grew up Shreveport, Louisiana, and I was always around Southern women, some stronger than others. I think there is certainly adversity in growing up in the South, and being a woman, and being a lesbian, particularly in the 60s and 70s. That was a difficult time, not just for women and lesbians. I think there are a lot of untold stories of strong women who were in the background. Everyone knew one of my characters, an aunt or a grandmother, or the lady across the street with a big sharp butcher knife, and their stories just never got told. They were too unconventional. They weren't the Auntie Mame type, and certainly not much for commercial success on the stage. So those stories just never got told, but we knew these people and knew they existed... they might have been a teacher or somebody who worked at the convenience store, the grocery store, the cleaners, or wherever, so I wanted to tell their stories, all our stories.

In addition to placing your plays in the South through stage directions, what makes them Southern?

What makes my characters Southern?

Characters or plays.

Well, I think from my point of reference, I was told "write what you know," and that's what I know. And I suspect really and truly that these characters could be from the Midwest, but I don't know their particular quirks. People in the South have particular quirks. I certainly don't know people in the Northeast, but the heartbreak, sadness, grief, they're all universal feelings. They're all universal emotions based on events that happen to people, but there's just a different way it's dealt with in the South. We have a little more humor in how we approach things, "let's sit on the front porch and have a glass of sweet tea and talk about it and you'll feel better, and if not, we'll make cornbread together." So, I think that's what I know and what I am comfortable with, and the dialogue with how people in the South express themselves. It's not real fancy most of the time. A lot of my dialogue is humorous. Folks have commented that "I don't believe I've ever heard anyone say that before."

Thinking of the detail in your plays, I have my favorites like the placement of the green stamps in Sing Me to the Other Side. What are some of your favorite placements of those quirks, props, and details?

Gosh, I'd have to think. *Sing Me to the Other Side* is based or centered on an actual historical event. Irma Lee is just a scream, and she's just as funny as she can be. She's kind of a no-nonsense kind of person. In many of my plays, there's food, there's a sense of hospitality, a sense of welcoming, and it's "come sit, let's have tea or let's have coffee or supper," and I think there's a sense of "this will make it better," or for a short time we'll just feel better because we will have had supper together or we will have had sustenance together and that between the two of us we can figure this out. I haven't read some of my plays in a while, but Irma Lee is a favorite character, full of spit and vinegar.

How did you decide that she would reappear?

I like the name Irma Lee, and I could envision her owning a bar, and you know, as time went on from that play [*Sing Me to the Other Side*] to *Waiting to Be Mended*.

In Sing Me to the Other Side, *you bravely and gently deal with some of the most difficult and violent history in the United States, and you treat even the most unlikable characters with dignity. From reading the play, and I haven't seen a production, I can understand how they got to where they are. How did you come to write about the Jim Crow South?*

PBS did a documentary in 2011 for the fiftieth anniversary of the bus burning in Anniston. I was very much intrigued by that. Then I purchased a book about the Freedom Riders. Having grown up in the South, I knew that not everyone is a bigot and a racist and owns a big white sheet and keeps a cross in the garage to burn on Friday nights and calls their friends to bring the kerosene. I knew people who were the complete opposite, who thought it was horrid and wrong, and some could speak up about it and some couldn't or dare not. They could lose their business, their lives. Janie Forsyth, whose folks owned the grocery store in Bynum, just outside Anniston, took water to the bus riders. The grocery nearly went out of business, and her life was somewhat in danger because of what she'd done. The explanation was, well, she was not quite right and didn't know what she was doing. So, the people of the community said, "you don't have to harm her, she didn't know any better, she just didn't know any better." But there were other people in the South that wanted to help and wanted that to be different, and I wanted to present that other side. And truth be told, there were more strong women who would stand up to that, who wanted to help, and let that be known, and risk what they could to make things right.

Could you speak about how you decided to end that play after this emotional and historical culmination? So, you've got an audience sitting there, and they are looking for closure or relief, and do they deserve that when you close that play?

Originally the ending was the phone call. It was left hanging. I talked to a set designer from one of the large theaters in Houston, mainly about set, costumes, and other things a playwright normally doesn't know much about, and she said, "you know, it would read much better, if you brought it back full circle. Can you bring it back to the beginning?" And I thought, well I can sure try. So, the way that it ends, you are back in a sense or at least in the same location as scene one. I don't know that a lot of people will go, "gosh, that ended so happy and a lot of people went home, and the world is a better place." I think it has a more realistic ending. It's not an *Easy Rider* ending. But there isn't really resolution for everyone. Gosh, some characters change, some don't, and to bring about resolution...maybe people can talk about how it ended and if it happened to you or if it were your sister, what would you be willing to do? How much are you willing to invest in solving this or in making it better or making it worse or keeping it the same. I would love to see a production of this. I've only had a reading of it, and it would be great to have a more formal stage reading, and goodness, a production would be the best, because that's the only way you can see what works or doesn't and "well that didn't make any sense, rewrite that part."

You have the same kind of circularity in Waiting to Be Mended. *Is that an intentional style?*

Probably not intentional. I'd have to look back to see how I ended some of these plays. Gosh, I'm trying to think. Well, I don't think so. I think it depends on the story and where I want it to go. With *Sing Me to the Other Side*, I knew how I wanted it to end before I knew much of the middle, probably very little of the middle, and very little of the beginning. I knew exactly how I wanted this to end. Well, that's not how it ends now. It was a phone call that initially ended the play. But after I developed the story, that's not how it needed to end. The others, I'm not sure, in *Waiting* [*to Be Mended*] I needed the good guys to win, I needed a resolution to the hate and to the prejudice. I need that or wanted that to prevail with this woman and what she was willing to do to make sure that this young woman was protected and cared for.

That play begins with a violet scene.

GF: Yes.

Could you speak to the inspiration for the beginning and what it was like to write that scene?

That being my first, first play, it was kind of "hold your breath and see what they do with this." The man who did a review of the play referenced that first scene as disturbing. I think I wanted to get everyone's attention really quickly from what was a very tender moment, from what was the innocence of a kiss, or the meeting in the parking lot, or that kind of thing, a little romance. Then to see the complete opposite, how offensive the kiss was to this man, and how far he was willing to go to express his contempt of it. It is a real attention getter, and no one left after that first scene. I don't think anyone left at intermission either.

In that scene, there's a kiss between two young women, Melissa and Claire.

Celia.

Celia. That is a scene is tender, and I also read it as symbolic of the truncated experiences of lesbians, significantly in the South. That isn't to say that people don't have meaningful lesbian relationships in the South or relationships devoid of external violence. I think that's brave and necessary to put front and center. A lot of lesbian fiction and film do not have happy endings, and I think that's a reflection of writers trying to reflect the trauma of living one's identity in a homophobic world. It's refreshing that there is a space for lesbian characters in your plays. Could you speak to how the maternal figure in that play makes safe space, in the home and in the world, for Melissa? The same dynamic arises with Lorean, the mother, in Sing Me to the Other Side, *as she makes space for Kate and Irma Lee.*

Glorie, the main character, in *Waiting* [*to Be Mended*], references how she felt that her sister was so mistreated by their own mother, because she did things differently and didn't toe the party line as it were. I think there was that sense, if it's not set outright, and I think it is in the play, that she didn't stand up to her mother and that she didn't care enough or protect her sister. And if she ever found her sister's daughter, by golly, come hell or high water, she was going to care for that child with unconditional love. And she was willing to pay the price, whether her marriage failed or whether she lost friends, friends in the church, to have this young woman feel safe and loved and cared for. And Lorean, I think, was just onery enough, and just a "devil may care" and "we're going to enjoy the day and what's wrong with that."

The same goes for the mother in Tattoos and Tater.

I can't think of her name, I'd have to look up those characters. People, if they can somehow realize, it's just about how people love one another. I don't think anyone sets out to determine who it is they love. I think it kind of sneaks up on you, and you figure out what flavors you like. And for people to be so blinded by the fact that it looks so different to them, or that they were told that it is different or it isn't right, or it's this or that, y'all need to put a face on these different folks. You know these people, and truth be told, you love these people, and you should love who they love. And don't make it any harder for them. I think I come from the underdog perspective, by golly, we're going to help these folks out.

The lesbian characters and/or people of color face an uphill battle in your plays, and a lot of these plays are set in an earlier time, and one of the forces they face is religion. Could you speak to the role of religion in your plays?

Sure, in *Waiting [to Be Mended]* it's up front and personal with Elmer's character. He's a deacon in the little local church, and by golly, he's against it because he's been told that women loving women is an abomination, and you'll burn in hell for that and probably if you know anyone like they might take you to hell with them. Wow, there isn't any place in the Bible where Jesus talks about homosexuality. So please hold your comments to yourself. Don't go there with me, don't tell me A, B, and C. If you'll look a little further, I want you to find that little spot in your book where that specifically says this is terrible awful. It doesn't exist. I think it's people's interpretation and I probably stepped on a whole lot of toes, but it's people's interpretation of that, and it's like, but that's your interpretation, and somebody else might have a different interpretation of how that's read, how that's incorporated in their life, how they love one another, how they support their community. So, let's all at least get a definition of terms as to what they mean. I think that religion has certainly harmed a lot of people, left, right, and center. You know probably more left than right and center, and it's hurtful, it's harmful, it's damaging. I think most of us who grew up in the 60s and 70s were terrified, terrified. I was probably more homophobic than many other people. You just need to keep your head down, and find a safe place. Go to X bar, Y bar, whatever it is, and don't be out amongst straight people. And the truth of the matter was it wasn't safe, it just wasn't safe. And not that people weren't strung up or beaten outside of the South, because we know they were, but there was a very valid fear. Don't let word get out. And we all had experiences where we were hollered at or threatened, if that's the very least that happened to us. You just knew there were places you didn't need to be. People didn't even need to guess or presume you were gay. And heaven help us if a bunch of us, and none of us looked like princesses or anybody that would go to the Miss America Pageant, we all stuck out like sore thumbs, were out where we didn't need to be. And we were just who we were, and how we dressed, and whether people appreciated it or not. It's probably good we traveled in a group so no one would come after us and some of us were bigger than others so that was a good thing too.

Did you ever witness any violence?

No, I can't recall that I did, but I know there were times when we were probably scared, that we knew it was time to leave. It wasn't a good place to be, or it wasn't a safe place to be. I didn't personally experience any violence.

It may seem like a thing of the past, for people or for your characters to remain in certain spaces to feel safe. But one of your plays, Old Spice, *is set in present time and it was censored.*

Yes. I'd have to look at the dates. It was 2015, maybe a little later than that. It was a sweet little ten-minute play, and one of the characters was a gay man, who meets a woman in a drugstore whose husband is in the hospital. She's getting shaving supplies for him. And she meets this young man who helps her, her name was Maggie, to secure the appropriate razor, and shaving cream, and perhaps even cologne for her husband, who obviously, as the play advances, is not doing well. It's a tender little moment that they have, and they're laughing and cutting up and talking about razors and different things. The company that did the production had a woman call and said, "we are making some changes to some of the plays, there are some bad words." I can't remember exactly what she said. It wasn't obscene, maybe just offensive, maybe that's the word she used, offensive. Well, I'm thinking it's swear words, cuss words, that sort of thing, and I don't have so much as a "damn" in that play, so well I understand. It's at the Fort Bend County Library amphitheater. The kind of thing you wouldn't want, goodness knows, to offend small children. So, I get it, I understand. Didn't think another thing about it. So, we went to the production. And I had told friends, and it ran for two weekends, to come see it, and we're sitting there watching the play and I went, "oh my God!" they've changed the dialogue, and this character is no longer gay, this young man. And they've cut that line and they've changed the other lines that don't make any sense whatsoever now that that reference is gone. I was stunned. Everything that I had ever learned, Dramatist Guild 101, don't let them change your dialogue. Don't let them change the words to your work. And it was so cavalier, I mean, that they did it and didn't say anything to me about that. It changed the entire meaning of the play. I thought that will never happen again. This will never happen again to me. So, I may be a little over vigilant about this now, even if an actor drops a line inadvertently. That did happen in a reading, and I thought, there goes that. But you can't change somebody's work. You just can't.

So, you consider that play to have not been produced?

No, because the original work was never performed.

Did you speak with them about it?

I didn't. What I did do was call everyone and say please don't come. It's a terrible production, it's not what I wrote, just please don't come. Don't waste your time. I think it was free to the public which was fine. You don't always have to be paid for your work sometimes to get out a little ten-minute play. I didn't even know how to deal with that. It was kind of too late to fix it short of pulling it. You could have done a cease and desist, hire an attorney, do that. But by the time you did that the little festival is over and they've already done it. But good God, it's not like there weren't gay characters on TV and in film, and surely, they knew in Richmond, Texas, that there were gay people. Even a gay man, for heaven's sake, it wasn't even a lesbian.

What are you working on now?

Well, I have a couple of plays that are just sitting in the closet so to speak. One play that's more on the front burner, is a work about an older woman who takes on the persona of Georgia O'Keeffe. It takes place in west Texas. Trying to figure out her journey to be somewhere else and be someone else. And how does she manage leaving the life that she currently knows to a life she's either imagined or dreamed of and what she hopes to accomplish and how she hopes to get there. And, yet not make it exactly about Georgia O'Keeffe but have enough references so that anyone who is familiar with that journey can go, "oh, well, this may not turn out well." And I don't if it's worth a two act play or whether it's simply a one act, how long to stretch that journey to make it compelling for people to want to sit through the whole ninety minutes.

You have something coming up in Texas?

Oh, I do, yes. We are waiting to get the contract. It's pretty much a done deal to do another production of *Shakin' the Blue Flamingo*. And Bonnie Hewitt, director/actor/theater administrator extraordinaire, reached out to me after the production in Houston in 2018 and said she wanted to direct it. And I've seen Bonnie's work and she's remarkable. She directed one of the most exceptional productions of *The Diary of Anne Frank* that I've ever seen. I never have to see another version of that. It was so well done and haunting and so compelling. So I went, "jump back, Bonnie wants to do my play!" So, she's on board. I hope to go down sometime in June to work with Bonnie during casting and rehearsals and to be able to work with the actors. She's very open to the playwright talking to actors. It's not like, "you go sit in the corner. You cannot talk to the actors. You must channel everything through me." So, I'm really looking forward to that and to the caliber of actors I know Bonnie will cast. The first production that we did was from a developmental program or project, and the women who were cast were a little older than is originally in the script which doesn't have to mean anything one way or the other, but this would be a little more in line with the character descriptions and age range.

Could you summarize Shakin' the Blue Flamingo?

Shakin' the Blue Flamingo is about a group of women, a group of lesbians, who went to college together who have decided they want to help put on an LGBTQ prom in this little Southern town. They're all in their mid-50s, grown up, working at different jobs. One's a counselor, one works at the car rental place. And some have stayed in touch and are closer to others and some not. A girlfriend from the past reappears and wants to reconnect with the woman she's loved all her life. And so, there's that dynamic of her pursuing this woman who's recently lost her partner. And of course, there's all the prom preparations and all kinds of emotions get stirred up and fired up, and tales of ex-girlfriends, and people who you thought you knew but it turns out you didn't, betrayal and intrigue and romance. It represents that place in time where it wasn't popular to be a lesbian when you were in college. I'd have

204 ♀ Sinister Wisdom 132 - How Can a Woman...?

to date it back to the 70s or 80s. It really wasn't popular then. We didn't have all our TV shows. People do live happily ever after. There's a long-time couple in the play who have held on and loved each other and they still dance and that type of thing. And the sense that even if you thought you lost your first love, that even if it didn't happen in that time frame, it's not to say it can't or won't happen. The commitment that Rosemary must find Mac, to rekindle it, no matter how long it takes. Love prevails in the end, and ain't life grand.

Do they go to prom?

That may be the sequel. I haven't thought about that. They might. They certainly had the outfits...the dress and the jacket or the fancy vest. I don't know, that may have to be another story.

Across all your work, do you have a favorite character?

I initially want to say Irma Lee. She's just kind of no nonsense. I think she has such confidence in who she is and who she's always been. And I don't think she was ever fearful or had to compromise who she was, being a woman who loved women. I don't think she was ever fear driven. And I think she had such conviction and sense of confidence that people didn't mess with Irma Lee. It was like, "hey, just leave her the hell alone. She's just fine. But don't introduce her to your sister." I like Irma Lee. And I have such tenderness for Mac. I think her struggles are overwhelming. And I love Rosemary because she is a woman on a mission. There are all kinds of similarities in my characters. There's a character in one of my short plays that has been the most produced, Jornada, that...I can't remember her name...she's very determined and very tender. She has such a tender heart to help and to want to make a difference and finds herself in the position that she can't and has a sense of sadness in that. I kind of like them all.

Do you have a favorite play?

Oh gosh, the play I worked the hardest on and that's taken the most time is *Sing Me to the Other Side*. I think because of the research that I did and the difficulty in trying to represent the characters fairly and not to write stereotypical characters of the South. We've all seen that and it's like, "and nobody talks like that. Y'all need to get a dialect coach. Nobody talks like that." And to present a fair portrayal of these people in '61 outside of Bynum, Alabama. And it was a hard time, and anybody who grew up then knows it was a very hard time for people just to make a living. And probably still today, there are hard times. Alabama is not a very economically vibrant state. I spent the most time and did more rewrites of this play. I worked with two different dramaturgs to try to get it right, to try to get it to be the best play I could present. I've sent it out to any number of contests and festivals. We haven't connected yet. But it may be my favorite.

Speaking of sending plays out and connecting with the right people, how has it been for you navigating the theater world and trying to get your work out, known, and produced?

Difficult. And I know everybody has difficulties. I think even today that there is, I think some of the theaters don't see any commercial success in plays about lesbians. Now they can tell you that they do have lesbian characters on stage, and in fact they do. And good for them. It is a small step. But they don't have plays specifically about, I don't want to say the lesbian experience, it's kind of a broad term maybe, but about regular, every day...these are the stories I know, and it's probably on my website, "women I know, women I've loved, women they've loved." This is about real people that I've known, and it's unfortunate that we are still not represented in our stories. And I think part of the problem is, like in many theaters, we're not at the table. We're not in the position to make the decisions about what's being produced. We are not the gatekeepers. And if you're not the gatekeeper, you're not going to get a place at the table. And when that will change, I don't know. I think I have better luck probably in smaller theaters that don't have such a high commercial risk of losing money on a play. But we've all seen terrible plays that you go, "I can't even believe it. I mean whose idea was it to put this on?" So, I know some of my work couldn't be any worse than that. There are just some bad plays. If it weren't for Bonnie, this play wouldn't be being produced in Houston. So, I've either got to find a director who is over the moon about my work, or I have to find an actor who has enough clout who is over the moon about my work, that they can go "Wanda Sue, I need your money, we're going to put this play on." More than anything, we need an advocate to say we need to tell these stories, and maybe it's not a commercial success. Maybe it's not something where we say we can move to France next year after we produce this lesbian play since we've made so much money. But enough so that you go, look, we're going to have to do that big, fancy musical to make up the difference because no, it's not going to bring the money in that you may want, but it will bring the people in. You know, we were talking about Jane Chambers back in the 60s, when she wrote *Last Summer at Blue Fish Cove*. Ruthann and I saw a performance in Houston at one of the churches, and it was packed. It was packed. And I went, "they didn't even advertise this in the paper." So, it's not that there isn't an audience. I truly believe there's an audience. It's not like folks are going to be like, "we don't want that many lesbians in one room." It's going to be more than just lesbians in one room to see a play. It's a universal theme, it's a great story, great characters, who wouldn't want to go see it. Maybe church people from a particular denomination, maybe them. But even then, they may have a lesbian sister. But it's hard and difficult. And so many of the gay theaters, or at least it used to be, with theaters having closed in 2020, but they primarily have male artistic directors. And I don't know really and truly if they are as interested in putting on a play strictly about lesbians, and oh, by the way, it might have a happy ending. We are not prison matrons, we're not prostitutes, and it's like, oh, those old stories, and they're never going to be happy, because, you know, they're lesbians.

If you could orchestrate the ideal production for one of your plays, which play, where, what theater, what region of the country, or any particular director would you choose?

I would love to have Bonnie do it, and then there's Ava DuVernay who does phenomenal work in film. I don't really know from a stage standpoint...I have a few friends who are wonderful and fine directors and who would probably do an excellent job as well. I don't know where, Atlanta pops into my head initially, maybe a little diverse. Some of the theaters realistically...I would say Texas, but no. There are wonderful regional theaters within the Texas area, but I don't know if it would be as well received as other places. Maybe here, Nevada, certainly California, the Northeast perhaps. I don't know, Minneapolis, that might be a good spot to have it produced. The best-case scenario is to have it get into a developmental project where you can have a reading or some kind of staged reading and then into rehearsal and have enough time to get it to that ready-for-the-stage place. That's what we did with *Shakin'* with Queensbury Theatre. We had a yearlong development. I mean that made a huge difference. It changed dramatically from the very first reading. You rarely get that opportunity. You have to either work with dramaturgs or actors or director friends to get it into the best format you know and then start submitting it because there aren't those opportunities like there were perhaps years, years ago for August Wilson or [Edward] Albee, or some of the others, Tennessee Williams. Lord, he could work forever on a play. But they had the time, and it was different then.

From your awards and productions, it's obvious that you are well known in Houston and throughout Texas as a playwright, what are your interests in connecting in this area [Henderson/Las Vegas]?

This is a tough nut to crack here. One of the theaters lost its venue during the pandemic. The other theater I think is, and I'm just guessing from a financial standpoint, needs to have more of a venue rental for comedy shows or such. I don't know that they're open to new works. You could approach them for some type of a staged reading, but again I don't know if that's their interest. There are too many other forms of entertainment here, certainly in the Vegas area than theater. Now, it looks like there's theater in Reno, smaller community theaters that might be viable to have a small production or a reading. There is a reading festival or contest up that way that was taking submissions. And certainly, theaters in California. But you just send your plays all over to whoever will take original works, and there are some that are LGBT themed which I fit right in to. But I think a lot of theaters are still very reluctant, regardless of the need to be inclusive and diverse and offer equality, to produce my plays. It's like "yes, we're going to write all about that on our website, but really, maybe not do it." And I think some of the problem is that the current people in administration, the decision makers, are like no, we don't want to be quite that diverse or quite that inclusive. We're just inching along to try to meet that goal, to try to fill that square, and it doesn't include you all.

When someone refers to you as Gwen Flager, award-winning playwright, what do you think?

Sometimes it's like I don't know who they're talking about. But realistically it's true. I have won some awards, and have been produced outside of Texas. I worked with an artist friend. We had great fun doing a performance about her and her work and her paintings. It's flattering and a part of it is just, "oh golly gee, is that who they're talking about?"

Is there anything you would like to share that I have not asked about your work or your life?

I think growing up in the 60s, when we talk about growing up in the South, it was terrifying to know that you were different. If I didn't know earlier than that. I would have never in a million years told you I'd be writing stories about lesbians. I think when *Waiting [to Be Mended]* came out, and it was selected in a reading series as one of six plays, I thought, "well, the cat's out of the bag now." Not that the cat hadn't been out of the bag. But I think it's the oddest thing to think of something that was so terrifying as a young woman could be, on the flip side, so fulfilling to write about, to talk about it and not be scared about it. Maybe that.

THE SECRET PARIS

Joyce Culver

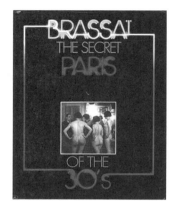

In 1977, as a newly enrolled photography graduate student at the Rochester Institute of Technology, I bought the book *The Secret Paris of the 30's,* by Brassai. I know the year that I purchased the book, as I signed it with my new name, JE Culver, and the date. No longer using my married name, I was in the middle of a divorce and an affair with a woman. The book was full of riveting images of night life in Paris in the early 1930s, and divided into chapters with captivating titles such as "Houses of Illusion," "Sodom and Gomorrah," "Lovers," "The Urinals of Paris," "An Opium Den," and "Ladies of the Evening," among others. Accompanying the very explicit photographs were stories by Brassai describing his night adventures and insights on the people he photographed. The social structure and culture of this very liberal city, along with quotes from his friends like Marcel Proust, Henry Miller, and Picasso also provided a crystal-clear picture. The book was a revelation to me as a thirty-year old woman entering a new phase of my life, and it has always been my favorite book.

Years earlier, when I was happily married, I had already seen one of the photographs in the book, and it scared me. In the chapter called "Sodom and Gomorrah," the photograph was taken at the lesbian bar, Le Monocle, and is a view from above of two women who are seated at a lovely table covered with a white tablecloth. The image creates a feeling that we are simply passing by their table, and are taking a look. The relaxed, well-dressed couple sits with two drinks, two plates, a pack of cigarettes, and straws around them. They do not look at the camera, and appear to be engaged with someone across the way, as we observe them. One woman wearing make-up, has pencil thin eyebrows typical of the time, and wavy hair. A spaghetti strap dress reveals her sparse cleavage as she leans in. Her hand is placed leisurely on her chin as she gazes ahead, uninterested in us. The second woman, clearly masculine, is dressed in a suit and tie. With a fancy twisted handkerchief in her suit pocket, her shoulder rests comfortably behind her partner, pushing her slightly forward. A no-nonsense expression on her face, the woman's dark, parted hair is cropped short and slicked back, and her manicured nails and hand rest casually on her partner's elbow. They both appear comfortable together. At first glance the couple appears to be heterosexual, but they are not. That they were women was alarming to me at the time, and why?

With my limited knowledge of same sex relationships between women in the mid nineteen seventies, the photograph confirmed scary thoughts about lesbians for me. If you were a lesbian, according to these photographs, the message was that one woman is masculine and one is feminine, leading me to believe that definite roles existed, with a need for lesbians to "pass" based on the heterosexual model. But for me, the bottom line was, I didn't understand it at all. Why was it necessary to mimic heterosexual society? But this is what I saw and interpreted from the photograph.

Le Monocle was a Parisian bar that existed in the 1920s through the early 1940s, and was owned by Lulu de Montparnasse, who insisted that butch women who came into her bar dress appropriately in suits and ties. Brassai photographed her too. In one image Lulu is gripping a cigarette at the side of her mouth, and leans in to smile at her feminine lover who is in a long dress and hat, sitting on a bar stool. The name of the bar was derived from the fact that a monocle, a single round eyeglass often worn in elite society, was also a signifier that you were a lesbian. The other signifier of the time was a white carnation worn in the lapel of jacket. But the bigger signifiers such as role playing and dress were distinctive: some women dressed as men while others dressed as women, and they appeared to be heterosexual.

Brassai, in his straight male candor, expressed his feelings about the masculine women, especially about their hair, stating, "And of course, their hair - woman's crowning glory, abundant, waved, sweet-smelling, curled - had also been sacrificed on Sappho's altar." His photographs, many shot with exploding flash powder sometimes held by an assistant, illuminated his subjects clearly in the darkly lit bars and balls. Anomalies were revealed. A photograph of chubby, masculine butchers, for example, who we might visit in their shops were an unlikely couple, smiling and dancing closely. Or a white rich woman, having arrived in a limousine, was shown clinging to a black man she desired, in another image. Brassai uncovered relationships that were hidden, revealing a secret society, and to me, the truth. As my new lifestyle evolved, I realized I had to find my own way, and role playing was not for me.

As I continued my graduate studies as a woman who was now separated from my husband, I found the only lesbian bar, the Riverview, located on the Genesee River in a seedy part of downtown Rochester. There I would see a variety of women, college types just like me, dressed in regular clothes, some with make-up, or without. Oh, there was one woman with shiny, slicked back Elvis-like hair who tucked her cigarettes into her rolled up short sleeve shirt. She fit the Brassai model of the butch.

My idea of a lesbian changed as I met women who did not fit the stereotype in Brassai's book. My year-long love affair with a woman who certainly passed as a heterosexual like me, changed the direction of my life. Looking back, Brassai's photographs awakened in me a fear around my own sexual desires, and I had no idea how that might look. Thrust into a new, startling social world, I needed to discover where I fit. I did not judge those women who chose to present themselves in ways that were comfortable to them, however. Brassai enlightened me with his photographs, and pushed me to look carefully at how I might express myself. My work from that point on as a photographer, completely changed. I began to value my thoughts and feelings which heretofore I had thought, could not be seen.

BEING A LESBIAN AT MERRILL GARDENS
Nancy E. Stoller

When I was a young woman in the 1960s, I was married to man for two years. He was Black; I am white. We had a daughter, Gwendolyn, who was born in Boston in 1968. I finished my PhD in sociology, I divorced my husband, and I got a job at the University of California, Santa Cruz. Gwendolyn and I moved to the Bay Area in 1973. It wasn't long before I came out as a lesbian, and for the next 45 years, I lived as an out lesbian. I was out at work, out to my extended family (who supported me, to my amazement), and out in the national news (because of a job discrimination case that I eventually won). I was out everywhere. Today, I think of myself as a lesbian.

Then when I was 75, I had stroke, which paralyzed my left side and left me disabled. What was I supposed to do? I had never married again, and had no long-term partner at the time. I had been independent for most of my adult life. After trying to make things work in my San Francisco home, where I had lived for almost 30 years, I found myself looking at assisted living facilities in Oakland, still in the Bay Area, but not on the steep hills that the changes in my mobility made impossible to navigate.

This essay is about my experience at Merrill Gardens, an independent and assisted living facility in the Rockridge neighborhood of Oakland, where I lived for two years before the lockdowns of the early pandemic made it into a fancy prison. In summer 2020, I moved to New Jersey to live with my daughter and her husband. Although I am a lesbian, my daughter will always be straight!

Discovering Merrill Gardens' Queers

When I was looking at senior living facilities, I always asked the person taking us around if they had lesbians there, was there any gay culture or anything like that. But no one seemed to understand what I was getting at. All they said was "we don't discriminate." I also looked around for other signs of diversity. I knew that some facilities had many black residents – after all, the place my former husband was living at in Philadelphia was majority Black. But no place that we saw in the Bay Area was very diverse – the Redwoods in Mill Valley was all white, even the staff was white; to say nothing of the community, which was predominantly white. They might have nice gardens or a nice view, but all the residents always looked the same and it was hard to tell just by looking who among them might be queer.

What did I want? Aside from some racial diversity among residents and staff (at least a few people of color somewhere, inside, or outside), I wanted the people to be like me (lesbian, radical, progressive) and to be out (rainbow, pink triangle, flannel, jeans, etc). That wasn't asking much, was it?

I couldn't live with all those white people in Mill Valley – and having to cross the Golden Gate Bridge would make it hard for my friends to come to visit me. Most of them lived in San Francisco or the East Bay. I couldn't drive anymore; would they go all the way to Marin County to come see me? I didn't know. As a single lesbian, with no spouse to care for me, my lesbian friends were my family of choice.

My friend (and ex) Molly had told me about a place that was all the way up in Santa Rosa that was specifically for retired gay men and women, but it required a very permanent commitment; you had to buy a residence to get in—no renting. It was very expensive and even further away than the Redwoods. The question of whether or not my friends would drive that far for a visit, coupled with my not being able to drive made it a non-starter.

Then there was Rhoda Goldman in San Francisco. I had heard that a few gay men lived there, but the community was overwhelmingly straight. Gwendolyn said I could afford it, and they did have a great art program, but there were a lot of old men with yarmulkas, which made me think it might be too Jewish for me. Plus, my mother had lived her final years there; it didn't feel right. Friends said the old men wouldn't notice me, but I was all too aware of them! Such was the decision-making process...

So, I decided to look at facilities in Oakland. On the same day, I visited a place called the Point, which was far too dark and gloomy, and I toured Merrill Gardens, which was only a year old. All things considered; it looked pretty good. There were about 100 residents in independent or assisted living, plus it had a memory care unit (which I had no need for). There was some visible diversity in residents and staff; there were women at lunch wearing blue jeans (I used that to assess the politics of the place); they had a one-bedroom apartment available; and the price was right. What could go wrong? Gwendolyn asked me about gay people.

"Oh, I'll figure that out when I get there," I said. And went off to spend the next three weeks getting ready to move.

Recently a friend asked me if I prioritized my racial identity over my identity as a lesbian. I think that is the trouble with some constructs of lesbian identity—the sense that one has to prioritize race over sexuality, or sexuality over race. I don't believe that one can be prioritized over the other. For me, the two are linked, intermeshed. One doesn't precede the other. You are born to them both. I can't be a white, culturally Jewish lesbian without being a lesbian who is not Black, or Asian, or Catholic. That's why one can't be prioritized over the other. I can't "see" myself without seeing what I'm not.

I asked Gwendolyn to call Merrill Gardens and reserve the apartment for me. The next day, we went back to sign the papers. I missed most of the fine details, just putting my initials on the paper every page or two. Gwendolyn would handle the payments. I am sure—I think—that this is what other people in a post-stroke situation like mine have done; relied on their friends and family for help.

This is what I found when I had moved and was settled in at Merrill Gardens:

Not counting the residents of the memory wing (like most residents, I knew little about the "Garden House") there were four Asian women and one man of Asian descent; I couldn't tell if any were gay, but I assumed all were straight. There was one African American man who was a closeted gay and one white man who was also closeted. All these people were in their eighties or nineties. One white woman, who was probably in her seventies, told me that she had aways had women as partners.

This is how I discovered the Merrill Gardens' queers.

One night, I saw a quiet dark-skinned man sitting by himself at dinner. My gaydar went off.

"Do you know any gay men here?" I asked.

He stared at me.

"Well, you look like you might know some," I said.

"No," he said, "do I look gay?"

"No, no," I explained before returning to my pasta, "I just said you looked like you might know some who are."

"I'd advise you to blend in the best you can."

That was his advice.

I kept eating and thinking.

Another pause ensued.

Then he said, "I can't think of anyone."

That was the end of our conversation.

Next, I tried sitting with a female resident and her friend at breakfast. Her friend, a white man, was waiting to eat breakfast with another resident. He had just told us a long story about a "friend" taking him on a train ride to Redwood City. Then he got up to meet his breakfast "friend." After he left, the woman told me that his "friend," a man, had spent the night with him.

Aha, I thought, *someone gay*. I asked her if he had ever been married.

"Oh, no," she said. "I really don't think so."

I went after the man and caught up with him at the mailboxes. He was over 95, wearing jeans and (what I learned later was) one of his many Hawaiian shirts. I had heard from another resident that when he was younger, he used to get up at 5 a.m. and run around Lake Merritt, but he didn't do that anymore.

"I'm wondering if you're gay," I said, launching right in. He looked surprised. "Because I am," I continued. "I'm a lesbian. I have just moved in and I'm trying to find other gay people who are here. Are you gay?"

Silence. But he opened his mouth. I could see past his red-rimmed eyes and his pasty skin, all the way back to his throat. Then he shut his mouth and smiled. From that moment on we were friends.

What did it mean? I thought it meant that he had grown up in a world where one never said out loud that one was gay, but he didn't want to lie to me, so he simply said nothing.

There was one other man, who was very closeted, but open with me, although I fought with, and about, him a lot. And one woman. When I saw on her list of friends and family, only women, "Oh," I said. "So, you're a lesbian."

"No, I'm not!" she protested. "I just prefer women."

Oh well, I thought. My reaction to most things I can do nothing about.

Most of the people that I met at Merrill Gardens were in their eighties and nineties. They grew up in an era of gayness that didn't speak its name. Everything was quiet. But their children and grandchildren are gay or fluid, and their great-grandchildren might even be trans. So, they were friendly towards me; they were nice.

As older folks, they're not homosexual or heterosexual; they're "post-sexual." And they didn't think I had a sexuality. Whenever I did talk about being a lesbian —and mostly I didn't—they were quick to tell me about their neighbors or friends who were gay. But not about themselves.

I didn't fit into their culture, which was heterosexual-normative, although they didn't know it. Instead of joining them in the post-sexual wilderness, I decided to make my own culture. I re-joined Old Lesbians Organized for Change (OLOC) and went to a retreat, and went to Mother Tongue Readers Theatre, although the latter looks down on the former. They call it politics, but it's class.

I'd have to make my own culture – because I'd be surrounded by straight people everywhere.

Being "Post-Sexual"

What does it mean to be "post-sexual?" I have given it a lot of thought and have tried to speak about it in conversation. In my opinion, it means going beyond the usual categories to discover what people really think of you. I am not a sexual, nor am I homo- or heterosexual. When someone looks at me, they might think "post-sexual" means the person is too old to have sex. But I think it is more complicated than that.

At Merrill Gardens there were some people who were still married. They lived with their husbands or wives. These people are heterosexual. Sometimes the husband was in memory care; then the wife made sure that everyone knew that she had a husband who was still around. There were a few single or widowed men, but most of the residents were women. And they were resolutely hetero, even if they didn't seem to have sex anymore. There were a few people who didn't spend time with their spouses during the day, but they always ate and slept together, or at least they lived in the same apartment.

The men who were alone and hetero just normalized themselves. They were like the guy who was offended when I asked if he knew any gay men. Or Joe, who moved to a different independent living facility in Alameda because the food was reputed to be better, but then came back with flowers and invitations to visit him but only if you looked like a femme woman. He had been unable to figure out that the person he ate breakfast with for eight months was a gay man, or that I was rejecting him because I reject all men.

Then there are woman residents who are women in their eighties and nineties, and who were waiting to die. These older women were all post-sexual. They had a sex life once but now it was behind them. At first, they included me in their world. I wasn't a threat to them because I was sexless, that meant we could be friends.

I felt kind of sexless because I was recovering from both a stroke and a break-up. I couldn't imagine having an orgasm with another person. When I went to sleep at night, I was in pain on my left side—I just wanted to rest. In the morning, I felt the same: my left side was in pain, I couldn't get out of bed, I had to swing my legs several times to sit up. I was torn between getting up and knowing that I couldn't sleep. Finding a lover who would put up with this seemed too hard to even begin. It would take a lot of talking and adjustment. I couldn't drive, I lived in senior housing, and I was surrounded by heterosexuals only adding to the feeling that a sexual life was in my past. I have since changed my attitude a little, just a little, thanks to the women at the OLOC retreat and to the authors of *Sinister Wisdom*.

These older women who were waiting to die took me under their wings and made me their child. Their children, grandchildren, and great-grandchildren were gay or trans. They themselves had moved on from their sexual lives, where to, I'm not quite sure. Some were heterosexual, some never married, all were friendly to me. I lapped it up.

Then there were the women in their seventies. Some of them were still heterosexual. No one would say she was gay or a lesbian. Three women I knew at Merrill Gardens found boyfriends after moving to senior housing. One woman had a boyfriend, whose wife of many years had recently died. They ate meals and slept together sometimes. Another found a man she liked. They slept together and ate breakfast and dinner together. The other women were not looking—or had stopped—I didn't exist for them. Maybe I sent out the wrong kind of vibes.

At Merrill Gardens, I never heard the word "lesbian" drop from anyone's lips. Not once. Maybe "gay" when talking about a grandson. "My grandson is gay." That's as close as they would come.

But they were nice. So nice. At least the people I became friends with. A lesbian friend of mine says it is like being white and assuming the privileges of racism. I think she is right about the privileges of heterosexuality. They looked down on me; felt sorry for me. But I felt sorry for them. Were we in a competition of who was the sorriest for whom?

One woman, who had never been married, invited me to go with her to eat pizza. She knew I didn't like to eat in the dining room. Another invited me to lunch; then after an hour of talking about herself, she told me her grandson was gay and waited for me to say something. But first she gave me all her credentials as a feminist and a heterosexual. I feel disgusted and used, but I knew she didn't see it that way.

At Merrill Gardens, I met an African American caregiver named Jayden who mentioned that "her woman," who she lived with, forgot her keys too—like me. Instantly, I knew she was gay. Then she told me she liked my mobility scooter. "Hey, I like your ride, especially this rainbow flag," she said and started to fondle it! She was the first person touch it like that: admiringly. "I like the rainbow," she said, while fondling the flag. I told her that I wanted to let everyone know that I am gay. She had to go back to working, but I knew I had a friend.

I went to Fern's apartment one day. It was dark, full of furniture, books, and papers. Fern sat on a brown easy chair, pulled back, with a bedside table beside her, strewn with medicines, half-eaten food, and more papers. Fern is severely disabled. She only left her room to go to the doctor, and for an occasional special meal. She seemed to have a caregiver with her all the time. While I was in her room, she told me about her problems. She had no interest in asking me any questions.

Suddenly, I realized that all the photos in her room were of women. "Are you a lesbian?" I asked. "No," she said, "I just prefer women." So much for that. Fern went on to tell me about all the problems she had with her last partner who left her when she began to get sick. (I would have left her too with all her complaining.)

All Fern's partners were women, no men anywhere. But no, she wasn't a lesbian. Was she afraid of the word? Maybe it didn't fit her. I'll never know because I didn't ask.

There you have it: two gay men and one half-lesbian woman. Out of 100 people or more, not counting the mysterious Garden House memory unit. That is why my lesbian friends and family are so important to me.

I realize at last that my friends are what people today call "curated." Most are "70s lesbians;" some are queer, others are straight or trans or gay or married. Even heterosexual, but at least they know they are. It all depends on when they became themselves.

I knew there was something wrong with the formulation: on one side were the heterosexuals; on the other were the homosexuals. It all looked equal.

It sounded right when my friend asked a young woman she had met, "Are you a lesbian?" The woman thought for a while and then said, "I am culturally, psychologically and politically a lesbian, but probably you would call me bisexual because I enjoy sex with men as well as women...."

But I believe that it is the behavior of having sex with women exclusively that makes one a lesbian. It is not a political choice. You cannot call yourself a lesbian and have sex with men. I have worked all my life to make it so being a lesbian in our society will be as easy as being heterosexual. This meant and continues to mean radical change is necessary, only then there will really be equality, everywhere. Not where heterosexism is dominant.

Maybe that young woman is a feminist. Maybe she still feels drawn to men. She might still be a feminist, but she is not a lesbian. Or is she?

The Weekend with OLOC

First, I had to pack and get ready.

Starting about a week ahead I began asking around for a ride with someone. Because I no longer drive, I knew I couldn't go without one, but hardly anyone was on the carpool list. "Don't worry," I was told by one of the organizers. "Most people don't register until the week before." So, I shut up and waited, although it was hard not to know how I would get to the retreat location. I had already found out that my friend Pat wasn't going. She would be in Chicago visiting her family. She had given me a ride before. Instead, I hoped for a ride with my friends Ginny and Susan, even though it meant that I'd have to listen to Susan talk about the history of American unions—which I am already familiar with – and I'd have to put up with her stop and start driving style. At least it would be a sure thing.

Why was attending the OLOC retreat so important to me? First, I had gone once before, and I knew what to expect. This means a lot to me. It makes it much easier. The swimming would be hard by myself, but I would find someone to help me. Second, I wanted to be around some lesbians, especially ones that act like actual lesbians, not like the married ones who live hetero-style lives. I wanted to be with women who dress in men's clothes or work in non-traditional jobs. My friend Cookie, who I went to college with, told me that she and her wife Marlene don't ever even think about themselves as being lesbians. Was I living in a past that no longer exists?

Then, a few days before the retreat, I heard from a woman that I didn't know named Terri. She would be happy to drive me.

Although I was grateful for the ride, I told Terri I didn't want to go during the afternoon rush hour to Napa. No problem, she said. I began thinking about bringing a sandwich with me for lunch, since we would have to leave before noon.

When Ginny checked in on Thursday, I told her I had a ride. She said (for the second of many times) that she was glad I was coming. I told her that, like me, Terri also used a walker to get around (something that was news to Ginny). I had learned that Terri used a walker when she had to walk a long distance, more than a block because she got tired. Ginny said she would call the organizers to let them know that I had a ride.

Terri was supposed to come before lunch, but later decided that 1 pm was better, even though it put us smack in the middle of the rush. I forgave her. After all, I was getting a ride and beggars can't be choosers. So, using only my walker, I lugged my small bag downstairs to the front desk and signed out. It was very hard to do on my own. Then 1 pm became 2 pm, and I called Terri several times. First, she explained that she called me (she had) to tell me she would be late, and that she hadn't answered any of my texts or calls, because she was trying to get ready and doing so would have only made her later. I was beginning to hate her even though we had never met. Then at 1 pm she arrived; she was a heavy-set African American and wearing a t-shirt with holes in it. All my well-repressed racism surfaced, but again I tried to keep quiet. She explained that she had a lot to do before she left, and the rush hour started in the morning anyway, so it didn't matter when we left, we would still hit traffic. Couldn't she have told me?

We arrived at the OLOC retreat, both needing to desperately take a pee, at around 5:30. No swimming today. The lifeguard was just leaving, and some people had gone for hikes. Laura, who was white and in her early seventies, helped us with our beds and then we ate dinner. The weekend began at the picnic tables. At about 6 pm. Terri hadn't brought anything for dinner. I was at one end of the tables, and she was at the other, wearing a loose dress. There was a lot of extra food.

Later that night two other Black women, a couple, arrived, they stayed in our cabin on the other side. Once they arrived, I pretty much ignored Terri for the weekend until it was time to go. Which is how both of us liked it, I think. The three of them came late to every meal, sat separately from others, swam together, and were the last to leave. I found them kind of exhausting, although I learned more and liked Terri better on the ride home.

The retreat had a schedule starting with breakfast at 8 am and ending in the evening after a salon of readings. Somewhere in the middle was time for a nap and a swim. On Saturday, which was the main day of the retreat, I participated in everything, and on Sunday, we were supposed to pack up our cabins at 12:30 or 1 pm, followed by swimming until 3 pm, then leave Hidden Valley right away. Again, I did everything on time, but we didn't leave until almost 4 pm because Terri wasn't ready. She wanted to visit as much as possible with the other African American women.

We were supposed to fill out a written evaluation of the retreat. I wrote on mine that the best thing was the pool, but I think my experience was a little different from others. First, I had to wait for a ride from my friend Susan to get to the pool, because I couldn't walk down the hill with my walker, it was too steep. Then I had to navigate the parking lot, which was on a slant. Then slowly, I made my way to the pool, wearing my bathing suit. I could see other women throwing some light balls back and forth. I wouldn't be able to do that – too scary, I'd need to hold on to the edge of the pool the whole time. Finally, after I had negotiated the path with gravel and flat stones (dry, fortunately) to the edge, I got to the stairs. I left my walker and my sandals there, held onto the banister, and started the slow process of getting wet. At first, the water was cold—as usual. Gradually, I got in, holding tight to the edge. Occasionally, I would swing, my feet coming up. That was scary but I persisted.

The nice thing was that people offered to help. "Would you like to grab my arm?" That was asked several times. I think that the women at the retreat were more familiar with aging. After all, these were the Old Lesbians Organizing for Change. They talked about it, as people at Merrill Gardens didn't, even though they were older. And the people at Merrill Gardens want you to help them. They don't want to help you.

I found that this super helpful attitude also extended to the meals at the OLOC retreat. I almost had to fight to put my own food on the plate that I had placed on seat of my walker to transport it from the buffet to the table. I felt that, even though I had limited mobility, I had to show that I could still get my own food. Then I could ask for help pouring water or juice or getting hot coffee with milk. In the dining room at Merrill Gardens, we had servers who brought the food to the table, so the residents are mostly passive, like diners in a restaurant, paying to be taken care of.

One of the things that I liked about the lesbians at the OLOC retreat were all their backstories. Heterosexual back stories are boring to me. The men go into the army; then they go to work. Their wives work at traditional female jobs like being a librarian, or a nurse, or a dental hygienist; then they get married and raise children. Lesbians, in contrast, tend to work non-traditional jobs for women, like being a finisher in construction; then they have one lover after another, unless of course, they came out late.

Their coming out stories are always of interest to me. One woman who I met at the OLOC retreat was named Louise. She lived next to a pond in Mendocino and had learned everything she could about dragonflies. I was one of six people to meet her on Sunday morning to see naiad shells and to learn about the 250-million-year history of dragonflies. She was fascinating. I just wanted to sit at her feet and learn from her. Another woman at the retreat was named John and dressed like a man. She was a public-school teacher for thirty years. A third woman had been in the Mother Tongue Readers Theater for forty years. Another one had started *Tradeswoman magazine*. All had interesting stories to tell. Stories that I wanted to hear.

One other thing that impressed me at the OLOC retreat was the evening salon—many of the women at the retreat were poets and writers. Some of them read from works that they had published in books. Others were good storytellers or singers. All of them talked about women they had known or loved.

Now, maybe the heterosexuals have pasts too. But do they talk about how they loved women? I don't think so. I was happy to hear lesbian talk. I was happy to flirt a little. And even though I was the most disabled person there, I was treated as a person. I was not invisible to these women.

Also, I learned that the women who attended the OLOC retreat all embraced their age, even the ones who were only in their sixties. They had the same ailments, like congestive heart failure, balance problems, or sleep-apnea, as people at Merrill Gardens. They have the same problems lifting things or opening a heavy door. They can also be cranky and demanding, just like older straight people.

And they love me as I am.

REMEMBRANCE

SKY-BLUE BOTTOMS
Evelyn C. White

In memoriam, Valerie Boyd
(December 11, 1963-February 12, 2022)

Manuscript five years late
Finds me hysterical
about the need to reach a Nobel Prize winner, a tempestuous
singer,
the estate of Norman Rockwell.
You (calmly) prop me up on every leaning side.
After all, you'd tracked Zora
delivered her to us exquisitely wrapped in rainbows,
Pray tell, what else would she wear?
Dusk
Finds me walking with you to a Georgia lake house,
I see fireflies for the first time in
fifty years.
You smile,
lace your shoes of sky-blue bottoms,
track the dancing light
And ascend.

Gloria Nieto
October 31, 1954-September 6, 2022

Kathleen DeBold
November 16, 1955 – October 9, 2022

It has taken me a year to remember and pay tribute to two dear comrades of mine, Gloria Nieto and Kathleen DeBold. I met both in the early 1990s working in the lesbian and gay rights movement. In activist LGBTQ activist communities, both were rock stars.

Kathleen DeBold was first an international human rights worker. She lived and worked for nearly a decade in Africa, then returned to work in the United States for the Gay and Lesbian Victory Fund, the Mautner Project, the Servicemembers Legal Defense Network, Lambda Literary, and other organizations. She was an organizer, fundraiser, and important queer leader, writer, and thinker.

She loved puns, word play, and lesbian novels. She loved most of all lesbian romance writer Barbara Johnson, her partner and wife of nearly fifty years. Kathleen was a member of the *Sinister Wisdom* board of directors early in my tenure. Together with an intern at Sinister Wisdom, we created the Notes for a Revolution blank book with quotations by women. Kathleen and I talked on the telephone regularly in the last years of her life. I miss her terribly.

Gloria Nieto was a leader in the New Mexico gay and lesbian community when I met her. She had a storied career as an activist including serving on the DNC and being the first out Latina lesbian to address the Democratic National Convention. Like Kathleen, Glo was a politico deep in her bones. She loved politics, queer politics, democratic politics, and all analysis of the structure of power and politics in our lives. We had many phone calls interrupted because Maddow was coming on. She never missed Maddow. Glo and I texted and talked every election night though she was talking to dozens, and I was usually just talking to her and hollering to my wife in another room. She had the best political mind and a warm laugh. In addition to politics, Glo loved dogs and cats and all animals and her wife and partner of over thirty years, Jo Kenny.

Kathleen and Glo knew each other. When Glo died after a long struggle with cancer, Kathleen called me urgently to send a note to Glo's wife Jo. In the months since their deaths, many times I have wanted to call them. Among other things, their pleasure at the Trump indictments would have been delightful. I have called other people instead, though I hold each of them in my mind and my heart.

This is a time of great loss for many in the *Sinister Wisdom* community. For me, these losses are resonant with the beginning of my career as a young person working in gay and lesbian communities when my brothers were dying regularly from AIDS. Death and loss never become easier; they continue to pile one on another, amplifying the loss. Kathleen and Gloria are two women I mourn, personally, and in community with everyone at *Sinister Wisdom*. Their memories as a blessing to me; their lives are a reminder to embrace the friendships of this lifetime and to always reach out and build new ones.

Julie R. Enszer
Fall 2023

BOOK REVIEWS

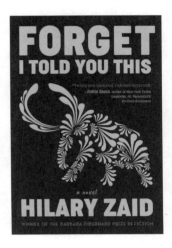

Forget I Told You This
By **Hilary Zaid**
University of Nebraska Press 2023
Paperback $21.95, 270 Pages

Reviewed by Judith Katz

Hilary Zaid's ambitious and prescient second novel, *Forget I Told You This*, is an adventure in the very near cultural future. Told by Amy Black, a grief stricken middle aged Jewish lesbian, her story is simultaneously a high-tech thriller, a Jewish family drama, and an edgy, sexy romance. Because Amy Black in an artisan who takes her work as a transcriber of letters absolutely seriously, *Forget I Told You This* is also an encyclopedia on the fading art of the scrivener. Throughout this story, Amy shares dozens of facts—about the history of the scribe, the materials she uses, and her place as a chronicler of the world. Amy is obsessed with the physical act of putting pen to paper, an art that is disappearing, and uses her craft to copy out letters for patrons who dictate them to her—to create beautiful artifacts of affection, love, and in one case, warning—embellished with beautiful, illuminated capital letters crafted from ephemera she has collected over time. She is rapturous as she describes color, light, the pleasures of vellum and multicolored hand-crafted inks. But she is also clear that she would like nothing more than a job making that art at the huge tech and data campus not far from her Oakland home, a fictionalized Google/Meta/X mashup called Q.

Here we are treated to the voracious appetite of Q's creator, M. David Hacker, aka Hack, an amalgamation of Mark Zuckerberg, Elon Musk, and Sam Bankman-Fried, who owns precious items—physical and data harvested simply for the privilege of owning them when nobody else can and destroying them, so nobody else ever will. Amy's quest to be employed by Q and her slow discovery of Q's mysteries and inner workings reads like a thriller. Zaid does an excellent job of replicating and satirizing the voracious greed of guys like Hack and reminding us that certain humanizing acts like putting pen to paper are vanishing over time.

Zaid has done a wonderful job of constructing, reconstructing, and de-constructing the high tech, steam punk, and culturally careless America we're living in today. We are treated to some hot and edgy sex scenes as Amy hooks up with the mysterious street performer, Blue through the social network, *SCIZR*, and we're introduced to a network of disrupters, outlaws, and rebels through Amy's restless nighttime meanderings.

But to my mind, where Hilary Zaid's shines is in her rendering of Amy Black's Jewish family. Amy's pianist mother is tender, gentle, and a little peevish as she tends to her stroke debilitated husband. Amy's adult brother has his own difficulties, but he is warm and generous and it is clear that Amy cares about him. They've become temporary guests in Amy's home while blackouts plague the Oakland hills and they're not unwelcome. They fill the space for Amy left by her longtime lover, Connie, and her traveling son, Tristan. There is real concern here, with lovely scenes of Amy, her mother, her brother, all taking turns nurturing and helping her father—to eat, to use the toilet, to walk across a room. For this reader, these domestic scenes were a comforting respite from the chaos Zaid depicts outside on the streets of Oakland, at the corporate campus of Q, and inside Amy's own longing.

If you are a reader who needs an entirely sympathetic protagonist, you'll have to cut this otherwise engaging novel a little slack. Amy's obsessiveness, her stubbornness, her naiveté, and yes, even her encyclopedic knowledge of all things scribe, made her a little annoying for my taste. But it was worth putting up with her as she led us through a really good story. And of course, she told us all about the *sopheret*, the woman scribe at the San Francisco Museum of Contemporary Jewish Art, whose job it is to copy out the Jewish Torah onto vellum paper—letter for letter, word for word.

Fire Dragon Street Theater 1962-1967
By **Jeri Hilderley**
Sea Wave Recordings, 2023
Paperback, $15

Reviewed by Roberta Arnold

Chronicling the life of an artist-activist much like herself, *Fire Dragon Street Theater 1962-1967*, in an engaging, fluidly-written plunge into the political subculture. Jeri Hilderley intertwines fiction with memoir in this new book. Lucina Holzer, an art sculptor in her 20s, grew up in rural Illinois and now lives in New York City. With a master's degree in sculpting, Lucina defies the dull art lessons she had been taught by a prestigious male art professor and follows her instinctive drive. In the first pages, she is forging a giant sculpture out of wood, "the size of a walk-in closet", both "rugged and handsome" (8), called *Rune*, a piece representing the muse within. With glances in the mirror, she describes herself working,

"Her tightly wound presence, awkward and serious, couldn't rest in a single reflection. She was changing shape as objects and people and nature did in the ripples of lakes and ponds" (9).

Lucina falls in love with a young male poet named Louis who lives on the lower east side, not too far from her own loft on Spring Street. Together they create a guerilla theater troupe made up of like-minded anti-war protestors whose intent is to educate and articulate their opposition to colonial oppression and the Vietnam War. The intensity of the 60s political realm is deftly illustrated in the characters' response to the seedbed of issues germinating and springing up across America. Lucina's reaction is visceral when she learns of the news of the freedom fighters: Chaney, Goodman, and Schwerner, brutally murdered by the KKK. She learns about Martin Luther King's dream and the fascinating uproar of the women's movement. We gaze through a real-time lens into the political strife. By turns, Lucina registers the vibrant response in her psyche. She remains tethered to her art and the theater group and Louis throughout the book, her internal voice fleshed out further by the author's own journals from the time. And while Lucina and Louis and their band of troubadours grapple with group dynamics, nuclear family issues, sexual desire and private anxiety, their need to speak activist truth against the systems of oppression continues rising to the foreground.

The book is neatly organized into time periods and telling chapters. Halfway through, we meet two lesbians involved in the women's takeover of a political underground newspaper similar to the takeover of *Rat Subterranean News* in 1970. The direction Lucina takes does not conform to a strictly lesbian narrative; instead, it is a complex interweaving of the lives of the counterculture voices that dared to defy socially prescriptive roles, the Vietnam war, and oppressions of sex, race, and class. The bubbling up of a lesbian story lies just beneath the surface in Lucina's love of her fellow troubadour, Marin. And when she meets another radical sculptor, one of the women involved in the women's takeover of the underground newspaper, it is short-lived. They meet at a local Spring Street bar, afterwards sharing a blissful kiss. The relationship ends there. Although Lucina senses something is missing in her sexual relationship with Louis, she stays with him through to the end. I'm guessing this lesbian interlude is a prelude to Hilderley's next book in *Rune Quartet*, as the author describes in the acknowledgments, "the next three novels will be the latest recording of my evolution" (453).

A compass for roads taken in the journey against injustice, this book describes the pivotal period of the 60s, spotlighted by the need to speak out and act. With the dexterity of a sculptor and the voice of a siren, Hilderley encircles the granular and the factual to reveal the provocative bloom of emergent political culture. It is a rare example of the artistic struggle of politics filled with lessons and insight. A gift given to us as an embrace, as the author's dedication reveals:

> I dedicate this book to everyone who understands that only through struggle, steadfast hope and tender revolutionary solidarity can we create the humane, just, compassionate, and non-violent world required to sustain our planet and all its living creatures—and to all the oppressed people who have found ways to express this unalterable truth with their own words.

Fire Dragon Street Theater 1962 - 1969 is a shepherding guide for artists, dreamers, and political activists alike who wish to work together in creative, activist collaboration.

Erase Her
A Survivor's Story:
How the Best Years of My Life
Were Stolen by Conversion Therapy
By **Cassandra Langer**
Paperback, 2023, $18.99

Reviewed by Roberta Arnold

Cassandra Langer's memoir *Erase Her* is a fast-paced delight to read, despite the horror stories. Langer unmasks a madman in charge of the reform school where she has been mercilessly delivered. A Freudian protégé psychiatrist and psychoanalyst runs the Quakerbridge school in the Catskills close to Sing Sing, where he also works, has Langer undergo conversion therapy to try to turn her from the tough, no-nonsense, spunky creative artist that she is to a femme-bot caricature. I am reminded of Harper Lee's Scout and all the tom-boy, tree-climbing, rebel characters in fiction whom I dearly love.

What sets *Erase Her* apart from the others is the deep dive into suicide that is so well-portrayed. Langer's artistic skills come into sharp focus as she paints an image of the teenage Sandy's despair:

It was a perfect afternoon when I crawled out of the window onto the narrow ledge that overhung the Croton River. I could glimpse the water through a thick canopy of green trees. Far below, the riverbank was lined with sharp gray rocks. I came out here all the time to escape prying eyes, because I knew that nobody monitored the rear of the house. I sat on the ledge and was startled by a sudden flash of color above me: a painted bunting in a puffy cloud. My thoughts fluctuated wildly. I wanted people to love me for myself. No one was standing by me. I was alone. There wasn't anybody I could confide in. I imagined my bones cracking, my neck snapping as if I was up in that cloud looking down, watching myself tumble off the ledge. I imagined bouncing off the trees and boulders on my way to oblivion. I imagined never having to feel like this again (145).

Thankfully, Langer did not jump. She became a pioneer feminist art critic with a postdoctoral fellowship from the Smithsonian. She has written about sex and gender in art in depth with many publications in magazines along with influential books such as *Mother and Child in Art*, *What's Right with Feminism*, *A Bibliography of Feminist Art Criticism*, *Feminist Art Criticism*, and *A Life: Romaine Brooks*.

Erase Her now gives us is a further reminder of what we could have lost if she had not been talked off that ledge by a fellow boarder at the nightmare of a reform school. I can't recommend this book highly enough, for its humor in trying times, and its gripping, vivid, detailed descriptions. The book would be best served as required reading in middle school. The threat to those trying to survive in schools that try to annihilate the many of us who don't fit the socially conforming mold is all too real today. This book is an antidote to that poison. It's the kind of book that when you pick it up you don't want to put it down, but if you do, you'll find that when you pick it up again it is like connecting with a friend that you haven't seen for awhile, because it doesn't matter, you are fast cohorts and allies, immediately on the same page again. Cassandra's Langer's memoir is a gift.

We Set the Night on Fire:
Igniting the Gay Revolution
by Martha Shelley
Chicago Review Press, Illinois; $27.99

Reviewed by Roberta Arnold

I leapt at the chance to review this book. I have been a fan and follower of Martha Shelley since she first became a gay activist back in the Stonewall era. When I first read her writing of political and personal events and experiences, I became firmly entrenched in my embrace. Shelley's writing is smooth, precise, funny, and wise. Sprinklings of traditional wisdom, tossed into the mix with revolutionary zeal, quench like the delicious tang of dried cranberries bedded into a hearty multi-layered salad, filling the heart with reverent joy: a delicious treat overall.

In the Introduction, Shelley writes: "At Passover we say, 'In every generation a new pharoah arises'—to oppress, to exploit, to murder us. The corollary is that in every generation we have to fight back. My hope is that this book inspires an army of younger generation activists to do just that" (x). Written in chronological order, each chapter lays out a concise story with thorough documentation. Shelley's paperback gem is 203 pages long with forty-three chapters. Each chapter takes readers on a journey where homespun anecdotes and pivotal historical events come to life with direct quotes, funny asides, and articles from the time period.

Shelley is a wonderful storyteller. One of my favorite chapters is "In Print and On the Road" where Shelley remembers, at the first Women In Print Conference, in Kansas, in 1976, when Nancy Stockwell "speculated that brown grasshopper spit could be harvested and turned into print ink" (172). Anecdotal nuggets like this one are recounted from a bird's eye perspective alongside, in this case, a quote from "Charlotte Bunch on Women's Publishing" in *Sinister Wisdom* 13 (Spring 1980).

In the Stonewall chapter, a *New York Times* article is referenced in the notes for those who want to follow along with that particular media account. Numerous other articles can be found in the back matter, along with Shelly's own notes about different chapters elucidating the roots of different political movements like the Gay Liberation Front (GLF), Gay Activists Alliance (GAA), Radicalesbians, Street Transvestite Action Revolutionaries (STAR), Third World Gay Revolutionaries, and Parents and Friends of Lesbians and Gays (PFLAG).

While this delightful book is history-centric, from the red scares of Communism to the radical organizations that sprouted up afterwards, it is also a profound example of memoir. The personal stories are so vividly depicted by such an adept storyteller (who knows how to throw a punch line) that I felt like I was witnessing events first-hand. If researching radical activism seems dull and boring to you, this book will turn your head around with its brash, funny, and concise recounting of a time period that was as wild and fun as it was historical. I have no doubt that this book will inspire fledgling activists who will read it, today, and in years to come.

CONTRIBUTOR NOTES

Abby Wallach is a queer Jewish woman currently studying at Williams College in Massachusetts. She's been a writer for as long as she can remember and started writing poetry as a junior in high school. She's interested in exploring how poetry allows writers to push the limits of language and believes that poetry is an important tool of both political activism and self-expression. Outside of writing, Abby loves to travel, read, and spend time with friends and family.

Alexandra Volgyesi lives in New York City with her human, feline, and canine companions, and is a coordinator at the Lesbian Herstory Archives in Brooklyn. She is a lesbian herstorian and recent Barnard College graduate. She enjoys participating in direct action activism, gathering together, and making short films. She is working on a novel.

Alix Lindsey Olson is an Assistant Professor of Women's, Gender and Sexuality Studies at Emory University (Oxford) and is co-director of Emory's Studies in Sexualities program. Alix's new book *The Ends of Resistance: Doing and Undoing Democracy* (Columbia University Press) will be published in 2024. Prior to Olson's academic life, she toured internationally for over a decade as a spoken word artist. Her poetry has been featured in HBO's Def Poetry Jam, Air America (with Rachel Maddow), NPR, *Curve* and *Ms.* Magazines, on Showtime's *The L Word: Generation Q*, and in dozens of poetry anthologies. Alix's work as an artist-activist is the focus of the multi award-winning documentary film *Left Lane: On the Road with Folk Poet Alix Olson* which traveled the international film festival circuit.

Allison Blevins (she/her) is a queer disabled writer and the author of *Cataloguing Pain* (YesYes Books, 2023); *Handbook for the*

Newly Disabled, A Lyric Memoir (BlazeVox, 2022); and *Slowly/ Suddenly* (Vegetarian Alcoholic Press, 2021). She is also the author of the chapbooks *fiery poppies bruising their own throats* (Glass Lyre Press, forthcoming), *Chorus for the Kill* (Seven Kitchens Press, 2022), *Susurration* (Blue Lyra Press, 2019), *Letters to Joan* (Lithic Press, 2019), and *A Season for Speaking* (Seven Kitchens Press, 2019), part of the Robin Becker Series. Allison is the Founder and Director of Small Harbor Publishing and the Executive Editor at *the museum of americana*. She lives in Minnesota with her spouse and three children. For more information, visit allisonblevins.com.

Alyssa Capri is a nonbinary lesbian and artist based out of Buffalo, New York. Capri has been painting professionally since 2015, shortly before coming out as queer. Capri has painted several public murals and published work both locally and internationally. Capri has been in a committed relationship with their partner for 5+ years. During that time, their partner has come out as trans femme and Capri as GNC Lesbian. Much of their work is informed by queerness, lived experience of family shunning, parenting, and the pursuit to live authentically and radically. Capri lives with their two children who also identify as nonbinary and trans partner, Honey.

Anne Haddox (they/them) is an artist of comics, fiber, and words living in Detroit, Michigan. Their art practice focuses on gender, place, and reclaiming craft as art. Anne's recent projects include SQUiRT, a queer erotica anthology, and a risograph-printed speculative nonfiction comic, CRUSH. They are currently exploring the powers of erotic needlepoint. Find Anne on Instagram @ annedrawscomics and @squirtzine.

Barbara McBane is a queer and disabled media artist, independent scholar, educator, and poet living on unceded Ohlone land in West Oakland, CA. An award-winning feature film sound editor, she has taught film, sound studies, queer theory, and gender studies at the University of California at Santa Cruz and Davis, the California College of Art, and at Ardmore Studios in Ireland. She is the former Head of Critical Studies at the Pont Aven School of Contemporary Art in Brittany, France. Her essays have appeared in *Art Journal*, *Film Quarterly*, *Film History*, the Leslie Lohman Museum's *The Archive*, and in film anthologies and art exhibition catalogues. Poetry is new. She has a PhD from the History of Consciousness Program at U.C. Santa Cruz.

Candace Walsh (she/her) is a creative writing (fiction) PhD candidate at Ohio University. She holds a fiction MFA from Warren Wilson College. Recent publications include *Vagabond City Lit, HAD, Roi Fainéant,* and *Beyond Queer Words* (poetry); *The Greensboro Review, Passengers Journal, Leon Literary Review, Craft,* and *Santa Fe Noir* (fiction); *New Limestone Review* and *Pigeon Pages* (creative nonfiction). Her craft essays and book reviews have appeared in *Brevity, descant,* and *Fiction Writers Review.* She received the 2022 Ohio University College of Arts and Sciences Teaching Assistant Award. Her poetry chapbook, *Iridescent Pigeons,* will be released by Yellow Arrow Publishing in July 2024. Her 2012 book, *Licking the Spoon: A Memoir of Food, Family, and Identity* (Seal Press) won the 2013 New Mexico-Arizona LGBT Book Award. Two essay anthologies she co-edited were Lambda Literary Award finalists. She co-edits *Quarter After Eight.*

Carla Schick is a queer social justice activist and educator. Jazz music has been a major inspiration in their writings & musings. They believe in the power of the creative arts to forge a path to transformative justice. Their works have appeared in *Forum, About Place, Suisun Valley Review, Journal X,* and online at *A Gathering of the Tribes* and *The Write Launch.* Their work was recently published in a chapbook of poetry about RBG (*When There Are Nine).* They won a poetry prize in 2023 from San Francisco Foundation/

Nomadic Press. They received their Certificate in Poetry from Berkeley City College, and served on the editorial board for Milvia St. Carla is a member of Circulo de Los Poetas, and Las Chingonas Poetas.

Cupid Maville is a non-binary lesbian studying Fine Arts at Nipissing University. Their art focuses predominantly on queer relationships, found family, and identity.

Deborah Seddon is a queer Zimbabwean poet, living and working in South Africa, teaching literary studies in English, mostly poetry, at the university currently known as Rhodes, in Makhanda, in the Eastern Cape. She identifies proudly as a lesbian. She came out late in life, after leaving and divorcing her husband. Since then, she has been determined to write more poems that are visibly queer. To celebrate the love, reckon with the damage, the waste, the long-term impact of familial and internalised homophobia. There is not enough queer writing in Africa. Compared to the United States, there is hardly any at all. She has also recently begun to write more about the complexity of being a Zimbabwean, following the death of her mother in Harare.

Deanna Armenti (She/Fae) is a Queer Genderfae poet, zine creator, and textile researcher in the Media and Design Innovation PhD program at Toronto Metropolitan University. Her research is practice-based and explores queer, kink identities through the lens of embodiment and affect to investigate the queer erotic form. Deanna seeks to combat the pathologization and stigmatization of the queer kink community through demystifying the lifestyle. Her creation of accessible material installations is an embodied practice which invites folks to engage with the community. Deanna's research focuses on queer temporalities, seeking liminal spaces and 'slices in time' as a means of conveying the non-linear spectrum of queerness. She also explores the community's use of signaling as semiotics, investigating alternate forms of communication such as sign based discourse.

Since January 2021, Dr. **Elizabeth S. Gunn** has served as Dean of the School of Liberal Arts, Sciences, and Business at Nevada State College (NS). With a concurrent appointment as Professor of Humanities at NS, she teaches Queer Literature and Women's Studies courses. She holds a PhD in Romance Languages and Literatures from the University of North Carolina at Chapel Hill and three Master's degrees: an MA in Spanish from Middlebury College, an MFA in Creative Writing from the University of Baltimore, and an MBA in Management from Johns Hopkins University. She is the author of numerous peer reviewed journal articles exploring the nexus of sexuality, citizenship, and visual culture. She also writes poetry and prose inspired by queer linguistics and the immutable awe of our natural world. Her most recent literary publication "Paralian" appears in Issue 25 of *Lavender Review: Lesbian Poetry & Art*. An avid runner and hiker, she lives with her wife and their three lively rescue pups in Henderson, Nevada, adjacent to the endless Mohave Desert.

Evelyn C. White is the author of *Alice Walker: A Life*.

Frida Clark is a Mexican-American lesbian working and living in Philadelphia, PA. She is an Aries sun, Aquarius moon, and Gemini rising. Growing up primarily in Richmond, VA, she favors swimmable rivers, but makes an exception for the Schuylkill. Her work mostly lives in her zines, letters to friends, and notes to her lover. Frida is deeply grateful for cherubs, stone fruit, and mollusks. Without queer archives and harm reduction communities, she would be lost.

Hadley Grace (they/she) is a lesbian from North Texas. They have used poetry to process their sexuality since realizing they were queer. As a young queer person from the south, Hadley Grace has experienced religious homophobia, external and internal. Today, they celebrate their identity and the identity of other queer people and lesbians. Through publication and performance, they have reached an audience of others working through the weeds of identity and self-acceptance.

Jan Phillips is a writer, storyteller and workshop facilitator who provokes thought and inspires action. Her retreats and presentations are multi-media, multi-sensory events that connect the heart and brain. She uses images, music, poetry and stories to evoke non-dualistic original thinking and expression. Jan is founder and Executive Director of the Livingkindness Foundation. She has published 10 award-winning books and 3 CDs of original music.

Janet Mason's book, *Tea Leaves, a memoir of mothers and daughters*, published by Bella Books, was chosen by the American Library Association for its 2013 Over the Rainbow List. *Tea Leaves* also received a Goldie Award. Her work has been nominated for a Pushcart Prize. Her novels *They, a biblical tale of secret genders* and *The Unicorn, The Mystery* were published by Adelaide Books. Her novel *Loving Artemis, an endearing tale of revolution, love and marriage* was published by Thorned Heart Press. She was last published in *Sinister Wisdom* 125: *Glorious Defiance*. She lives in Philadelphia with her partner Barbara and their new cat Peanut.

Jenny Johnson is the author of *In Full Velvet* (Sarabande Books, 2017). Her poems and essays appear in *American Poetry Review*, *BOMB Magazine*, *The Georgia Review*, and *The New York Times*. Her honors include a Whiting Award, a Hodder Fellowship, and a NEA Fellowship. She is an Assistant Professor of Creative Writing at West Virginia University, and she is on the faculty of the Rainier Writing Workshop. She lives in Pittsburgh.

Jessica Dittmore lives in Philadelphia with her spouse and two perfect children. She travels the country as a mitigation specialist, working on death penalty appeals. A cartoon of her accomplishments would show Bb wearing a sash with merit badges: grew up queer in the Midwest (before the internet!); BA and BFA from the University of Michigan, Masters in Social Service from Bryn Mawr College; Absurdist; Amateur Do-Gooder. Hobbies include studying economic theory and navigating the impossibilities of parenting in the United States. See more of her art and poetry at www. instagram.com/jessica_dittmore.

Joyce Culver is a photographer and educator living in Greenport, New York. Before the pandemic she resided in New York City, and in her forty-year career there shot portraits, celebrities, and taught photography at the School of Visual Arts and Nassau Community College. Beginning with her early portraits in the LGBTQ community in the 1980s and 90s her use of photography serves to reveal social aspects and her personal feelings. Permanent collections include: the Amon Carter Museum, the International Museum of Photography at the George Eastman House, MOMA, and are in numerous private collections. Publications include: *The Arc of Love*, *Butch/Femme*, *Exploring Color Photography*, *Forbes*, *Fortune*, *Newsday*, *The New York Times*, and *Art News*, among others.

Judith Katz is the author of *The Escape Artist* and *Running Fiercely Toward a High Thin Sound*. She co-edited *Sinister Wisdom 119: To Be a Jewish Dyke in the 21st Century* with the late Elana Dykewomon in 2021.

Kathy Anderson is the author of the novel, *The New Town Librarian* (NineStar Press, 2023), which features a middle-aged lesbian librarian in search of a new life, and the short story collection, *Bull and Other Stories* (Autumn House Press, 2016), which won the Autumn House Press Fiction Prize and was a finalist for the Lambda

Literary Awards and Publishing Triangle's Edmund White Award for Debut Fiction. She lives with her wife in Philadelphia, PA. To connect: kathyandersonwriter.com.

Kimberly Dark is a writer, sociologist and storyteller, working to reveal the architecture of everyday life so that we can reclaim our power as social creators. She's the author of four books, including *Fat, Pretty and Soon to be Old: A Makeover for Self and Society and Damaged Like Me: Essays on Love, Harm, and Transformation*. Her essays, poetry and stories are widely published in academic and popular publications alike. She teaches for Cal State Summer Arts and travels to offer keynotes, workshops and lectures internationally and online. Her topics include social inequality, social transformation and the role of appearance and identity in our everyday lives. Sign up for The Hope Desk newsletter at www.kimberlydark.com.

Kristy Bell is a Navy veteran, writer, photographer, and poet who returned to the deep South in late 2018 after a 22-year hiatus. She frequently writes about carving her own space within a region that holds tradition so closely. She has work in *Snake Nation Review*, *Hallaren Literary Magazine*, *Bull Literary Magazine*, and *Rivanna Review*. She lives on a farm in southwest Georgia, with her partner and a menagerie of animals. Find her on Twitter at red_dirt_poet.

LauRose Felicity an elder sex positive lesbian femme who loves lesbian butches! Something that apparently remains controversial. In the 80s (though she faced daily risk of violence as an attorney for battered women and raped children) she was defamed as a femme because she wasn't a "serious feminist." She founded The Portal: A Lesbiqueer Museum and Archive in Ashland, Oregon in 2022. She is a mother and grandmother from when lesbian mothering was illegal, a builder, an artist, and the delighted lover of Penn Hart, my long sought butch herband. She was a queer family law attorney and teacher when outing was disbarment, firing or even arrest. She helped found, and record, lesbiqueer rights and culture because 'we cannot live without our lives.'

Lily Kaylor Honoré is a lesbian poet and writer from San Francisco. She is currently an MFA candidate at NYU where she teaches undergraduate creative writing and the fiction co-editor of Washington Square Review. She held the 2020 William Dickey poetry fellowship at San Francisco State University. Her work appears or is forthcoming in *Michigan Quarterly Review*: *Mixtape*, *Foglifter*, Stanford University's *Mantis*, and *Through Lines Magazine*. Honoré lives in San Francisco and Brooklyn with her cat, Angelica.

Lindsay Rockwell is poet-in-residence for the Episcopal Church of Connecticut and hosts their Poetry and Social Justice Dialogue series. She's been published in, Connecticut River Review, Amethyst Review, Iron Horse Literary Review, Willawaw, Birmingham Arts Journal, among others. Her collection Ghost Fires is forthcoming from Main Street Rag Press spring/summer '23. Lindsay holds a Master of Dance and Choreography from New York University's Tisch School of Arts and is an oncologist.

Liz Ahl is the author of *A Case for Solace* (Lily Poetry Review Books, 2022) and *Beating the Bounds* (Hobblebush Books, 2017), as well as the chapbooks *Home Economics* and *Talking About The Weather* (Seven Kitchens Press), *Luck* (Pecan Grove Press), and *A Thirst That's Partly Mine*, which won the 2008 Slapering Hol Press chapbook prize. Her poems have appeared in numerous literary journals, most recently in *Revolute*, *New Verse News*, *TAB: The Journal of Poetry & Poetics*, *Moist Poetry Journal*, *The Lickety-Split*, and *Porcupine Literary*. She lives in Holderness, New Hampshire. Find out more at https://lizahl.com/

Llywelyn Lee is a Welsh poet whose work focuses on mental illness, queer identity, and the divinity in the every day. They have been published in the likes of *Velvet Fields*, *Poetically*, *Grime Prophet*, and *Saving Daylight*. You can find them taking out too many library books and feeding street pigeons.

Marlee Alcina Miller (she/they) is a multidisciplinary artist with a special focus on writing and performance. Her work explores the dreamscape, love in all its many forms, and radical vulnerability. She attributes a large part of her artistic influence to dancing with her queer chosen family, Audre Lorde, writing her signature love letters, Nikki Giovanni, and crying while sipping wine in the shower. Marlee Alcina is pursuing an MFA in Narrative Nonfiction at the University of Georgia. She is the author of the chapbook "Mommy Issues; Poems for the Fragile, Queer Heart." Their writing has also appeared in previous issues of Sinister Wisdom: A Multicultural Lesbian Literary & Art journal, and Solstice Literary Magazine.

Mary Vermillion is a Professor of English at Mount Mercy University in Cedar Rapids, Iowa, and the author of three mystery novels. The first, *Death by Discount*, was a Lambda finalist in two categories: Lesbian Mystery and Lesbian Debut Novel. Learn more about Mary and check out her blog, *Midway*, at maryvermillion.com.

Almost thirty years ago, in 1995, **Minnie Bruce Pratt** connected lesbian identities, trans lives, women's liberation, and a revolutionary future in the groundbreaking *S/HE* (Firebrand Books; reissued Alyson, 2005). Those lyrical and sexy vignettes will return from *SW* in 2024-25. This issue's selections are from Pratt's sequel, underway, *Marrying Leslie*.

Monica Barron is a founding member of Lesbians WriteOn. Her book of poems, Prairie Architecture, was published by Golden Antelope Press (2020) after poems had appeared in *Poecology*, *Naugatuck River Review*, *The Chariton Review*, the anthology *Times of*

Sorrow, Times of Grace, ArtWord Quarterly, Briar Cliff Review, The Lucid Stone Poetry Quarterly, Rosebud, and *Ecotheo Review.* She is the Nonfiction Editor of *Wordpeace*: A digital literary and art project dedicated to peace and social justice and is a certified yoga instructor working on bereavement programming with Hospice of Northeast Missouri.

Nancy E. Stoller was Professor of Community Studies and Sociology at the University of California at Santa Cruz. She is the co-editor of *Women Resisting AIDS: Feminist Strategies of Empowerment.*

nerissa tunnessen (they/them) is a jewish dyke and dancer/choreographer/educator from washington, dc currently residing in philadelphia, pa. a graduate of Vassar College with a BA in history, nerissa is passionate about connecting historical research and art to work in a space of understanding communal emotion and the human experiance. their recent work has explored topics of historical and present-day women's spirituality, gender identity, sexuality, mourning, community building, and the complexities of empowerment. nerissa is influenced by their natural surroundings and is fascinated with revolutionary eroticism and communal love.

reuben quigg (he/she) is a transsexual dyke and writer located in central florida. the inspiration for his work comes from lesbian history, the natural world, and her passion for intersectionality and social justice. writing is his passion and she is currently working on a long-term collaborative project with her partner. you can follow his work on instagram under the handle @otterjaws or contact her through email at reubenquigg@gmail.com. "doing it butch" is her first published poem.

S. C. Gordon is a British writer and editor whose first poetry collection, Peckham Blue, was published in London by Penned in the

Margins in 2006; her second collection, Harbouring, came out in November 2015 under Math Paper Press in Singapore. Her poetry, fiction, and non-fiction, and translations have been published in journals anthologies such as United Verses (2014), Unsavory Elements (Earnshaw, 2013), Middle Kingdom Underground (HAL, 2011), Unshod Quills (2011), Junoesq (2015), Eunoia Review (2020) and The May Anthologies 10th Anniversary edition (2003). As a literary editor, she has worked on the English translation of S. P. Tao's memoir, as well as Fan Wen's 'Land of Mercy' for Rinchen Books. She is a founder of Literary Shanghai, and is commissioning editor for the online journal Alluvium. She holds a PhD in Comparative Literature, and is a mother of two.

Taylar Christianson is a trans butch poet from western Washington State, where they are working toward a BA in creative writing. They are the author of two self-published chapbooks, and their work has appeared in *Sweet Tree Review*. Their poetry tends to return to patterns of viscera, fabric, repetition, junk, the corporeal, and women with problems. In their spare time they can be found watching vampire movies, reading Eileen Myles, and walking in the fog.

Sarah Sarai is author of *That Strapless Bra in Heaven* (Kelsay Books), *Geographies of Soul and Taffeta* (Indolent Books), and *The Future Is Happy* (BlazeVOX[books]. Of *That Strapless Bra*, Spencer Dew (*The Aliites*, Univ. of Chicago Press) wrote, Sarai "presents world of distractions, represented here by forks in mattresses, the undeserved fame of snake, and the need to kill various elves." Julie Enzer wrote, "Sarai brings poems that fuel a long ride." Sarah received a 2023 micro-residendency in poetry from N.Y.C.'s South Street Seaport.

Serrana Laure (she/her) is a queer writer germinated in New Mexico, grown in New York City, & currently planted in San Francisco. Her work has appeared or is forthcoming in the *North Da-*

kota Quarterly, X-R-A-Y Literary Magazine, Red Noise Collective, Big Bend Literary Magazine, Silver Rose Magazine, and elsewhere. She holds an M.F.A from Sarah Lawrence College, and teaches writing remotely and in person.

Susan Spilecki teaches writing at Northeastern University and MIT. Her poetry has been nominated for the Pushcart Prize and published in such journals as *Frontiers, Quarterly West, Quarter After Eight, Potomac Review, Midwest Poetry Review*, and the 2023 anthologies *Beyond Queer Words* and *Swagger: A Celebration of the Butch Experience*. More at www.buildingapoem.com.

Suzanne DeWitt Hall (she/her/hers) is the author of *Where True Love Is Devotionals;* the *Living in Hope* series, which supports the family and friends of transgender people; *The Path of Unlearning* faith deconstruction books; and the *Rumplepimple Adventures*. Her debut novel *The Language of Bodies* (Woodhall Press) launched in October 2022. She is mildly obsessed with vintage cookbooks and the intersection of sexuality and theology. Suzanne lives with her beloved transgender husband, two terriers, and a cat named Chicken. Her work is designed to shine the light of love into hearts darkened by discrimination and fear.

Urszula Dawkins (she/her) is a writer and editor living and working on unceded Wurundjeri and Boon Wurrung country in Naarm/Melbourne, Australia. She is co-creator, with Alex Nichols, of A Thousand Threads | Thousand Threads Press, a collaborative and peer-led writing initiative for trans, genderqueer, and non-binary folk. Thousand Threads Press has produced two books, *We Twinkle Like Gold* (2022) and *In Flux: Trans and Gender-Diverse Reflections and Imaginings* (2022). hello@thousandthreadspress.com.au

Zoe Cutler is a multimedia weirdo based in Detroit, Michigan. Her work has been described as "Itchy and Scratchy meets James

Bond" and "Can you write something easier for once?" Her primary instrument is the trombone, but during the pandemic she pretended to be a whole brass quintet on YouTube. She publishes her compositions via Zoe's Sounds Publishing and many are available at ZoeCutler.com. In her free time, she tries a new hobby each week, from brewing to ceramics, in the hopes that someday something will pan out and she can quit trombone once and for all.

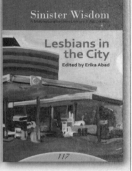